Wind in the Clouds

C. J. Canady

Wind in the Clouds

C.J. Canady

Copyright © 2023 Christopher Jacob Canady

All rights reserved. This is a work of fiction. Names, characters, places, and incidents either are the products of the author's imagination or are used fictitiously.

Any resemblance to actual persons, living or dead, businesses, companies, events, or locales is entirely coincidental.

This book or parts thereof may not be reproduced in any form, stored in any retrieval system, or transmitted in any form by any means—electronic, mechanical, photocopy, recording, or otherwise—without prior written permission of the publisher, except as provided by United States of America copyright law.

For permission requests, write to the publisher at phantasmalhorizonbook@gmail.com

Library of Congress Control Number: 2023907383
First Edition ISBN: 9798842741014 (Paperback)
ASIN: B0B2VGZ73B (Digital)
Cover art by leraynne
Edited by Belle Manuel

This book is dedicated to Halle Bailey. (Yes, that Halle Bailey).

Though you may never read this book, my intentions are pure. Windy Breeze and Ariel would be best friends in an alternate universe.

Contents

Title Page
Copyright
Dedication

Lilian	1
Chapter 1: Windy	7
Chapter 2: Windy	12
Chapter 3: Windy	20
Chapter 4: Nigel Cloud	26
Chapter 5: Nigel Cloud	33
Chapter 6: Leopoldo	39
Chapter 7: Windy	41
Chapter 8: Windy	47
Chapter 9: Leopoldo	50
Chapter 10: Windy	53
Chapter 11: Windy	59
Chapter 12: Leopoldo	68
Chapter 13: Windy	71
Chapter 14: Nigel	78
Chapter 15: Nigel	86
Chapter 16: Windy	92

Chapter 17: Nigel	100
Chapter 18: Nigel	108
Chapter 19: Windy	116
Chapter 20: Nigel	123
Chapter 21: Windy	131
Chapter 22: Windy	138
Chapter 23: Nigel	145
Chapter 24: Nigel	153
Chapter 25: Windy	161
Chapter 26: Nigel	170
Chapter 27: Nigel	177
Chapter 28: Windy	183
Chapter 29: Rhyanna	185
Chapter 30: Leopoldo	188
Acknowledgments	191
Author's Note	193
About The Author	195
Of Thorns and Hexes	197
Cosmic Threads	199

Lilian

Golden sheets of sand pelt the crystal carriage I am in, obscuring the entrance to the temple in its tumult and exacerbating my anxiety with its ominous, ceaseless pattering. Squinting my sleep-heavy eyes, I peer through the sheets of swirling, glittering gravel. The Matriarch's carriage has come to a halt, unicorns collapsing to their knees, exhausted. The journey here was exceptionally long, taking days upon days to find the temple. I could've sworn the Matriarch had informed all Zepyterians she and Namanzi had a special connection. This connection was so strong it afforded the Matriarch the keen ability to locate the Goddess's Temple in the vast expanse of the Gnobi desert. Perhaps Namazi and the Matriarch aren't as close as they once were because, undoubtedly, the Goddess would've revealed her temple's location days ago.

    I have no room to complain, though. I've been a prisoner of Zepyteria for two months too long now. My crime: stealing loaves of bread to feed my family. I am, in a sense, the Matriarch of my family, and I did what I thought was right. Had I known I'd be apprehended and locked away, I would've been sneakier about it. I've always been cat-like in my thievery, but I had been in a rush.

    My siblings and I were starved for food, and Iman's Bakery threw away perfectly fine bread. Instead of donating it to the hungry, the stubborn baker tosses the food out as if the Realm hasn't experienced food shortages semi-annually. Iman must've caught wind of what I was doing, as well as hundreds of other food-poor citizens because on that fateful day I decided to dumpster dive... I was apprehended by Keepers!

Amana. Akeesha. Abdul. They are all I have. I'll do anything to return home to them in one piece, even if that means becoming a servant of Namazi—as the Matriarch put it. So, to shorten my six-month sentence for stealing bread, I agreed and was rewarded by becoming a servant of the Goddess. The Matriarch promised this trip would be "short and sweet." Yet nothing is close to "short" or "sweet" about this.

I really, really shouldn't whine. I pray I am home soon to see my sisters and brother. Although we're half-siblings, and I don't share their unique names, Mom's dying wish was I protect my siblings by any means necessary. And I will. I've written several letters to Amana—the eldest behind me—and delivered my writings to her by my carrier Pidgeon. A small ice bird I swiped from the Matriarch's menagerie.

Lupin, my name for him… or her… I can't really tell, hides inside my heavy cloaks. Pinned between Lupin's beak is a letter I've written for Amana.

I have this unnerving gut feeling I'll never return home after today. As much as I try to shake away the stirring sensation within, it wraps its cold arms around me and squeezes tight. It's because every Fairy on this journey knows the Matriarch's secret. And it's a secret she undoubtedly wouldn't want to return to Zepyteria, that's for sure.

We, servants of Namazi, a handful of Keepers surrounding the Matriarch for dear life, the Matriarch's cook, and her personal Healer, spill out of the carriages into the blistering sun and the soft, itchy sandstorm brewing.

Kernels of sand sprinkle my lashes and sting my chapped lips. Using one hand as a shield from the elements, I turn my head this way and that, unable to find the temple.

Then, as if a veil has fallen away, the temple of Namanzi flickers into the here and now. The stone walls, a deep pearlescent cerulean shade, undulate as if the Waters of Namanzi thrive in and through the structure. I am mesmerized and awestruck this Goddess's home has seen no aging or decay.

Didn't the Goddess Namanzi roam the Fairy Realms a

thousand years ago? Shouldn't the temple reflect such passage of time?

All my questions evaporate soon after. The stone guards, erected at opposing sides of the entrance with battle axes and war hammers, are—

I gasp. What is this? Why are those things there?

My gut instinct is to run, to fly away from this... this...

"Have I gone mad?" one of my fellow servants of Namanzi asks. "W-Why are those beasts at this sacred temple?"

The Matriarch snaps her fingers, and a Keeper, one of her sword-wielding servants, glides over. "Matriarch Xenobia cannot and will not entertain questions at this moment. Please refrain from speaking."

"I don't like this at all," another servant says. "I-I want to go home. Please. This feels wrong."

"Kill her!" The Matriarch's words are final and followed through by a Keeper. I turn my head and plug my ears, but her scream is enough to haunt me until the day I die.

And that day is today.

"Gather 'round." The Matriarch's Keepers group us, servants, into a single file. "Should you protest, should you run, should you dare even think of betraying me, you'll all end up like this one." The Keeper holds the poor Fairy's lifeless head in one gauntleted hand, brows twitching, mouth open in a silent scream.

"No!" A servant breaks free of the formation and flies up and up, sand pelting her beautiful wings. An arrow soars through the air, whistling the name of death. It strikes her, and she comes crashing down to the hard-packed earth with a crunch.

Panic blossoms its head, weaving through us servants as the true nature of this voyage comes alive. Here I thought this was a pilgrimage to pay respect to Namazi, but this is far worse.

I must update my letter—the Matriarch has more secrets under her skirts than I realized.

I break away from the line; a Keeper moves in to strike. I

raise my hands in defense, and my stomach empties on his ironclad feet.

"I-I'm not running..." I cough between breaths. "I-I need to lie down."

"We've no time for that!" he shouts, yanking me up to standing and forcing me back into the queue.

We move forward, the temple soon swallowing us inside her domain. I scan the ancient and unfamiliar writings etched into the fluid walls. Had I paid attention in Ancient Fairy History class, I'd probably have been able to decipher most of this scrawl. But I can put two and two together. And it does not add to what I had always been taught about the Fairy Realms.

The figures safeguarding the temple are Realm-shattering clues that tell me everything I've ever believed in is a lie.

We are taken down a winding passageway, rivulets of water lapping at our toes as the strange inscriptions on the walls descend to the floors. This passage soon yawns into a chamber: massive and sparkling with Namanzi's water. I nearly overlook the impluvium at the center. The sun peeks through the compluvium, illuminating the secrets beneath. My knees lose strength, and my stomach turns upside down as dead, hollow eyes peer back at me. Hundreds of dead, hollow eyes.

Matriarch Xenobia saunters in her skirts of pinkish-gold up a short flight of water-stairs with her Healer by her side. When I glance up to where they've settled on the landing, there are two figures at the apex. The center figure, an unmoving water effigy, makes my jaw drop—is that Namanzi's actual form? However, it's the moving figure that captures my full attention.

"My love." A masculine voice comes from the shadowed figure. He steps into the light, his features obscured by his dark robes. A brief flash of his canines makes my breath catch. "It is time to restore the lands back to their—"

"No," the Matriarch says breathlessly. "I cannot forgo my powers just yet."

"Do not renege on our deal, Jordana," he says, extending

his hand—a lime-colored hand—with long black fingernails to touch the Matriarch's stomach. "Forsaking Nasturtium of rebirth will cause cataclysmic results. It must be done for the sake of *my* Realms."

"These Realms are not yours," Matriarch Xenobia grumbles, face strained as her Healer aids her to the ground. "These Realms will one day belong to me."

"They belonged to us first!" he hisses.

I gasp at my realization. I must tell my sister about this.

"It's time," her Healer says.

Time for what? I begin to think when the Matriarch screams. It's time to reveal her secret. And her secret became scarier.

I still myself amongst the screaming and the panicked looks plastered upon the faces of my fellow servants and the Keepers. Seeking a way out, I steal a glance over my shoulder. The exit is clear for me to break free.

I do on the umpteenth scream the Matriarch produces. If any Keepers are following me, I pay them no mind.

Sprinting for my life down the pathway, I search my pockets for my quill and slowly wake Lupin, murmuring in his sleep. I'm scratching away at the letter, adding more and more details, when, for some reason, the Matriarch's screams that had faded away in the distance comes roaring back to life.

I'd run in a loop.

A Keeper grins at me, his lips visible through his visor.

There's a gasp of relief, then another softer cry—a baby's cry.

Her secret is out.

"Now!" the Matriarch shouts.

Keepers storm up the stairs, encircling the cloaked male. Swords swinging wildly, missing their mark. The Matriarch, her Healer, and the new bundle are whisked away by Keepers, wings outstretched to carry them out through the compluvium.

"I should've known better." The nameless figure laughs, the noise jarring, serrated like a blade forged from hellfire.

5

"Brothers! Sisters!" A horde of shadowy figures leap out like phantoms and begin attacking the Keepers, cutting through their armor as if made of paper.

The dots align, and the pieces to this awful puzzle slowly fall into place. But I have no time to write any of this, to share this with my sister. Instead, I focus on the closing compluvium, casting darkness in its wake. Servants take off for the only exit above, wings beating as fast as my heart. But the water comes alive, resembling a many-legged creature that steals the servants from the air and plunges them deep within the waters below. Their bodies thrash for an instant before succumbing to their ultimate fate. I must be quick if I hope to deliver my last message to my sister. Because in the next coming moments, I'll be dead.

I peck Lupin on his head and release him.

"I love you, Amana. Akeesha. Abdul. Goodbye."

A servant screams as a Keeper drives his sword through her gut, uses his foot to kick her off his sword, then advances to the next servant. Then the next, before flying to the safety of the desert world outside.

A Keeper advances on me, sword glinting in the sunlight. I shut my eyes tight and pray to whoever is out there to save me.

But my savior is far too late.

Chapter 1: Windy

Clink!
Clink!
BANG!

  And... I'm done. Go me! Tinker's middle leg—more specifically, her tibia—is all fixed by way of my mechanical expertise. I've constructed a lightweight titanium prosthetic leg for my favorite Dragonfly. So, when Tinker goes off flying to... wherever she goes late at night, she'll always have a safe landing. Tinker lost her middle leg on one of her midnight rendezvous and gave Mister Ed and me a good fright when she crashed through the roof of our home during supper about five months ago. It took me four weeks of digging in the trash mountains in Junkyard Canyon—my home—to find material that wouldn't weigh her down.

  "I'll be back, Tinker." I nudge her on her turquoise frond. She flitters her wings excitedly and presses her frond against me. I am afforded a glimpse into her mind—which is still a mystery to me—as her eagerness to leave overwhelms me.

  "Not so fast, there." I gesture to Puff-Puff—my balloon Dragon—floundering about in a thick brown mud puddle to cool off. "Puff-Puff and I think you should stay another night to rest up. We wouldn't want you to make a crash landing in Ogre territory, now, would we?"

  Tinker's ever-flittering wings, buzzing with anticipation, are reduced to a whisper as she bobs her head in understanding. She pulls away from me, our shared connection divvying. She makes a sound like a whimper and stalks to a trash heap, offering the promise of shade from the blazing forever sun—a glittering red-orange ball in the crystal blue skies.

I'm still amazed by the sun, its warmth. Its life-giving energy. I remember the first time I saw the sun eight years ago when I was freed from my life imprisonment beneath the Palace of Zepyteria. All I knew for my first eight years of life were the cold stone walls of the prison and the crystal beams that kept me confined like a caged animal at a bazaar. That was all I knew.

Imprisonment.

I was left in the dark about why I was there, an infant, then a young Fairy, cut off from the world beyond until the day Mister Ed came to my rescue.

"Who are you?" I had asked when my bleary eyes popped open at the sounds of footsteps and wingbeats. I scrambled to the corner of my cell when Mister Ed looked at me: his eyes, blank, white as snow, peered at me from behind the crystal beams. "Don't hurt me!" My wings, slashed and ripped by the Keepers following the order of Matriarch Xenobia, rippled shockwaves of pain through my being as they fluttered open, thinking I may be in danger. My fight-or-flight response.

"I'm not here to hurt you." Mister Ed's gentle timbre gave me pause; my heart skipped a beat. The lilt of his voice and that broad smile pressed upon his wrinkly face dotted with sunspots presented me with something I'd never had before: kindness. With his membranous wings bleating a *crunch-crunch* sound as they slowed their pace, Mister Ed dipped his head to me and introduced himself. "I am Edward Breeze, known as the Junkyard Fairy to all the Fairies of Zepyteria."

Mister Ed shifted his baggy, brown cloaks to reveal a golden shillelagh under his right palm, swirling magical colors I had never beheld. He tapped his colorful stick on the cement. Yellow sparks of light danced from beneath his cane and swirled up the groove-like veins etched deep within the wooden stick as if carried by a soft breeze. Mister Ed removed a crystal device from his cloak and set it atop his cane. The crystal sparked to life, and a wavering image of someone startling familiar was projected forth.

I remembered that face. Those soft honey-brown curls, that heart-shaped face. Those shimmering green eyes and that deep earthy skin. And then she spoke. And I remembered who it was. Madeline. I had forgotten all about her. I thought she was a mere dream I conjured in my mind because all I knew was the prions and a deep, hollow loneliness.

"Dearest, sweet girl, who I've only known for such a short while," Madeline said, her voice like a song, "By order of Matriarch Xenobia, I must aid the Matriarch and her band as we traverse the Gnobi plains delivering offerings to the Temple of the Water Goddess Namanzi."

Madeline continued, "If you are seeing this message… it probably means the worst: I haven't made it back safely to be with my husband or you, our newest edition to the family. I have cared for you since you were born." Her green eyes mist over; a personal memory has caused her to fall silent for three to four slow breaths. "I cared for your mother before she was to be… Never mind that. It is your third birthday, and I don't want to sully this marvelous occasion with unwelcome news. Now, it is time for you to see the Realm of Zepyteria—" Madeline was distracted. Someone called her from afar. "Be good, my sweet Windy."

The projection then ended, and Mister Ed reclaimed the crystal. He straightened his spine as he peered at me through his fog-laden eyes. "I'm six years late, Windy, by no fault of my own. I promise you that. A girl your age should be outside, exploring, frolicking about with Fairy-like whimsy."

I did not know how old I was. I had no clue when I was born or that I had a mother. I barely remembered Madeline. If it weren't for her voice, I honestly would've thought she was an illusion I used to cope with this life I was cursed with.

I looked down at my tight fists, crumpling the sack of a dress I was given by a Keeper who pitied me because I had nothing else to aptly cover my body and released my grip. "I have a name?" I asked, unbelieving that I deserved the peculiar name Madeline had bestowed upon me.

I wasn't sure I liked it yet.

Mister Ed said, "Yes. We all have names. Incredibly unique names."

I wanted to tell him otherwise, to share the horrific names I'd been called all my life. Names I thought belonged to me. Horrible, vile… Normal. The Keepers would hurl insults at me, some using their feet or fists to express their distaste for me. For something I had no control over, for something I am innocent of.

"So, Windy," Mister Ed said as he tapped his cane in a slow rhythm, "are you ready to go home?"

"Home?" Speaking that odd word weighed heavy on my tongue. "Home," I said again. "I… I don't know what that means."

Mister Ed chewed his lip before answering. "A home is a personal sanctuary where you are afforded a place to rest and just *be* as you are." He pondered for a moment, then shook his head. "It's impossible for me to accurately tell you what a home is since I've always had one. Whereas you, Windy, have only known this as your home—" he gestured about with a shaky hand. "But this is not a home: this is a soul-crushing abyss that an innocent soul like you should've never been subjected to. Would you like to go to your new home, Windy?"

Windy? I scrunched my face up at him. Then remembered: *Oh, right, that's me. I guess.* I'd have to get used to that name. Windy. What does it mean to be Windy?

I gulped down a lump in my throat before I spoke, too overloaded with what having this new name and having a home meant. "I… I'm hungry." My stomach, empty for two days too long, grumbled something fierce that made Mister Ed jump. I was used to it: starvation. The Keepers would taunt me with morsels of food until I'd pass out from sheer exhaustion. They'd never let me die, though. Even when I was on the cusp of death, they'd toss me a loaf of bread and a cup of water so I could live long enough to face another beating.

Mister Ed chuckled to himself. "Well, let's get you out of here so you may have a delightful meal in your belly." Mister Ed smiled at me; his teeth as white as his eyes. "I want to make you a promise." He palmed a hand over his heart. "If that's alright with you?"

I shrugged.

"I promise you'll never know darkness again. All your days henceforth will be filled with sunshine, laughter, and love. Is that all right with you, Windy?"

Chapter 2: Windy

My wings. My ever-healing wings, forever enraptured by the past trauma inflicted on them by the Keepers, are my constant reminder of who my parents were. Of the horrors they and their band of thieves caused Zepyteria. My parents were the leaders of the Clepsydra, also known as the Water Thieves. They sought to destroy the Realm of Zepyteria and overthrow the Matriarch to claim the blessed Waters as their own. In their attempt, they failed. They were captured, locked away under the Palace, and tortured. And soon, I was born to a mother bound by her wrists and feet, with her wings clipped so she would never fly again.

"*All we wanted was Water...*" Those were my birth mother's last words before she was executed. Those words have haunted me every day since I read about the Water Thieves and their failed crusade.

Blessed by the ancient Goddess Namanzi, water is the most sought-after resource in all of Nasturtium—the collective name of the five fairy realms—after the waters evaporated to nothingness thirty years ago. Zepyteria is the only Realm where the blessed Waters thrive, where not one Fairy will ever suffer from dehydration.

My wings are the tomes, bold turquoise fabulists that shout lies to my fellow Fairies of Zepyteria about who I truly am. They're hyper-aware of who they think I am because of who my birth parents were, but they don't know me. They don't know Windy. If they did, they'd think I was a pretty cool Fairy to hang out with. That's if they'd ever give me a chance.

At least I have Puff-Puff, I think as I gaze at him through my floor-length bedroom mirror, gnawing on a chew toy—a rubber ball—he unearthed in the Junkyard. Puff-Puff has been with me forever. My littlest Dragon was rummaging around the Junkyard, hunting for scraps to eat when I was freed from prison. Mister Ed tried to shoo him away, but I told my new Dad I knew what that feeling was like and asked if the little Dragon could join us for dinner. Mister Ed was apprehensive because baby Dragons don't stay so small for long. And yet, eight years later, Puff-Puff is still that same balloon-size he was when I first met him. Mister Ed and I think Puff-Puff has an abnormality that keeps him small and cute. Whatever it is, I'm happy he's never outgrown me, never flown away to be with his family wherever they are.

On my crystal pink vanity that hovers above the floorboards sits a recycled plastic container of stinky green salve I dab on my wings to hasten the healing process. Now, I've lived in Junkyard Canyon pretty much all of my life and grown accustomed to the smells that come with the junk, but this stinky green mush nearly knocks me dead every time I use it. This green goop once belonged to Ms. Madeline, who'd use it on her patients whenever they found their wings injured.

Ms. Madeline was a famous Healer who everyone adored. It was why the Matriarch requested Ms. Madeline to aid her and her band on their journey to the Temple of the Water Goddess Namanzi. Matriarch Xenobia, being the embodiment of grace, love, and unselfishness, looked to proffer a contribution to the Water Goddess to prolong Zepyteria's boundless blessings of water. As claimed by Matriarch Xenobia herself, she's said time and time again that Namanzi has chosen her as the *"Golden Fairy."* This means the Temple of the Water Goddess only appears to the Matriarch alone.

Who knew Gods and Goddesses were so picky…?

Unfortunately, on Madeline's pilgrimage to the Temple, Ogres attacked the Matriarch's caravan. Ms. Madeline and many others were…

I wipe away the threat of tears teetering on my lashes. I never had the chance to get to know Ms. Madeline. And Mister Ed was never afforded a proper goodbye.

Upon final inspection of my slow-healing wings, I will them away with a thought, and with a *whoosh*, they slip between my shoulder blades.

"Windy." Mister Ed calls for me. He's in the pantry, from the sounds of plastic bottles clattering to the floor.

That stubborn old man couldn't give me five extra minutes to clean myself before rushing to make brunch. Mister Ed has been acting weird all day, and it's not his *usual* weird. This weird is more of a skittish-panicked weird. He's been tidying up the house—something he never does. He even bought fifteen air fresheners from a local smell-goods shop yesterday. He has also instructed me to wear my best fit tonight: my cozy sunflower yellow dress and kick-butt, knee-high boots speckled in mud.

"A little help would be nice!" More clattering noises bound through our tiny two-bedroom home.

"I'll be right there." I gather my blueberry-dyed locs, heavy with undried water from my much-needed hot shower and wrap my hair into a bun. I glance over my features: my brown eyes, exhausted with lack of sleep after long days in the sun, and my brown skin aglow like a bronze statue that's been finely polished. My tapered ears perk up when there's yet another crash from the pantry. What the Puff is Mister Ed so panicked about?

Could it be…? Does Mister Ed have a date coming over?

A slight grin moves my lips to one side as I rush to meet Mister Ed. In the hall, I race past Ms. Madeline's pink-crystal key that Mister Ed had said was the "Key to her heart." The Matriarch delivered it herself to Mister Ed, commemorating his departed wife. I kiss my fingers and tap them on the glass container where the key spins in endless revolutions for some unexplainable reason. I offer Madeline my love… and I sort of mentally think-say to her, *"I hope you're not the jealous type."*

Mister Ed has been so alone for so long, and I think it's swell he's put himself back on the market. If Mister Ed has someone else to pester, he'll be less nag-y and happier and—

Oof!

I'm on my backside, my feet dangling over my head, knees by my ears. Propping myself on my elbows, I search for the cause of my fall: twenty plastic bottles of spices strewn across the dining room floor, rolling in various directions. Puff-Puff assesses me, twisting his entire balloon-body left and right as he coos his concern.

"I'm all right," I say, wincing from the hurt as I pick myself up.

"Ah, there you are." Mister Ed, draped in his famous cloak he never removes, glides to me, wings beating leisurely, with his shillelagh in one hand and a tiny bottle of black sea salt in the other. "I found it, no worries. Now I can add some zest to the brussels sprouts."

I can't help but roll my eyes. All this calamity for brussels sprouts? Seriously! Those nasty baby cabbages are so gross and flavorless. I am offended for Mister Ed's date. She'll be disgusted by the smell alone. I know I am.

Using a long, wooden paddle, Mister Ed removes a piping hot glass bowl from the clay oven.

Disturbed by the sizzling green balls of tightly compacted leaves drizzled in butter and reeking of sulfuric stink, I blink at Mister Ed. "Um... is it okay if I have brunch at Sid's? Besides, it looks like you're expecting company."

Mister Ed's silvery hair is slicked back, and his raisin-dyed beard is nicely trimmed.

Yup, Mister Ed has a date coming over.

Mister Ed's snowy eyes widen slightly. "H-How'd you figure?" he asks, sprinkling the black sea salt atop the cabbage. He's a little too heavy-handed with the seasoning. My stomach flips upside down.

"I... I wanted it to be a surprise. I hope you're not upset with me about it."

I blow a raspberry. "Oh, please. Why would I be upset?" Patting him on the shoulder, I peck him on the cheek. "Mister Ed, I'm happy for you—"

"Y-You are?"

"Yes. I mean, hello, you need to get back out there. I'm sure Ms. Madeline wants you to find love again?"

"Huh? Wait... I think you're confused—"

Scooping Puff-Puff in my arms, I say, "I'll be back before the fourth sun shower."

The Realm of Zepyteria experiences eternal sunshine and frequent rains. We Zepyterians—well, those far older and wrinklier than me—have said the moonrise, and the light of the stars, was quite pleasant and the perfect time to slumber. But Quill, the provider of moonlight, revoked Zepyteria's right to its ghostly white splendor shortly after Matriarch Xenobia revoked Quill's water privileges. Add to that water-less list the realms of Crest, Abethia, and Luxon.

Matriarch Xenobia, as it is written in her lovely scrawl in the *Zepyterian Antiquity Volume Three*, believed the Quillians unworthy of the blessed Waters, for she has a personal divine connection to Goddess Namanzi. Being the mouthpiece of the Goddess Namanzi, the Matriarch can giveth and taketh the most precious resource away.

"Wait." Mister Ed calls for me as I open the front door.

I pause: one foot out, one foot in. A figure clad in stone-gray Keeper armor, readying their gauntlet hand to knock on the rickety door, casts their gaze down at me through their visor. Hardened silver eyes regard me as a pest to be squashed.

My body stills, entangled in a mass of horrific memories. The Keepers. Their swords slicing my wings to tatters. Their iron fists striking my face, my ribs. My blood spilling on the stone floors.

On reflex, I drop into a crouch, with Puff-Puff squeezed so tight in my arms he struggles to free himself. A hand lands on my shoulder. I stiffen as tears well in my eyes.

No! No! No!

"You're fine, Windy." Mister Ed's face breaches through the terror-filled memories. His voice and comforting hand break the spell. I looked up at him, watery lashed.

"How long will you have your Matriarch standing in this

squalor?"

Through my cloudiness of tears, Matriarch Xenobia, robed a pink tulle gown, adorned with a halo of shimmering crystals atop cropped sunny-blonde hair, saunters her way to the threshold. Her royal amaranthine wings, glossy in the forever sun, spiral with fuchsia and hints of purple. The Matriarch is breathtaking: eyes the colors of ripened peaches, skin like a fragile porcelain doll. With a flourish of her tulle, the Matriarch looms before me, backlit by the sun—a corona of warmth enveloping her.

"Forever Sunshine, Windy," she says, her voice mellifluous, sweet, and inviting.

I bow my head in return, showing my utmost respect for the Matriarch. Bowing her head to me in the most gracious manner that makes my heart skip a beat, the Matriarch then says something that makes my ears burn.

"Your father has requested my presence here today in this Junkyard. I would've declined the invitation because royalty like me would never deign to travel to such a... home like this. However, due to the nature of my relationship with Madeline Breeze—" at the mention of Ms. Madeline's name, the Matriarch kisses her fingers in oblation. "—I took Edward on his offer to pay *you* a visit. Edward has written to me constantly about how you'd be the most enticing garland for the coming merger between Quill and Zepyteria. Exciting, is it not?"

The Matriarch lost me there at the end with the whole merger thing. I only say one thing to her amongst the hundreds of other questions I've always longed to ask the Matriarch. "So... you're not Mister Ed's date for tonight?" It's a stupid-stupid thing to ask, but it makes total sense to me because Matriarch Xenobia cannot be here to see *me*—a Junkyard Fairy.

And my stupid-stupid question is met with a parade of laughter from the iron-clad Keepers to the Matriarch herself. The Matriarch's face is pinched tight as she guffaws a throaty noise; it's as if she's never laughed before. Ever.

"Edward," the Matriarch says as she strips a piece of fabric from her ruffled sleeves, "you haven't shared the news with her, have you?" Dabbing a glimmer of tears on her waterline, she *tsks* her annoyance at Mister Ed. "Shame on you, Edward."

"I... I should've told you, Windy." Mister Ed's voice is shaky with hurt and worry, and fear. What does he fear? What the Puff is going on? Why is he behaving all... Wait!

I replay the Matriarch's ramblings in my head. *You'd be the most enticing garland for the coming merger.* Garland? GARLAND!

"Mister Ed," I choke on my tongue as realization dawns on me. It's as if a bucket of ice-cold water has been dumped on my head with the metal bucket in tow. "You're giving me away to be married? Are you insane—"

Mister Ed parts his thin lips to speak, but the Matriarch interjects. "Why, yes. Isn't it lovely?" the Matriarch claps her hands giddily. "Marrying a Prince is every girl's dream, is it not, Edward?" She sighs. "Why, oh why, do you believe Windy should be considered? Aside from her beauty, I'm not too impressed with her wardrobe choices nor her lack of formal education."

I stare at Mister Ed in disbelief, face twitching, fury jittering through me. Why in hell's bells would he even conspire to do something like this behind my back? He, of all Fairies, should know how much I love the Junkyard, how the Junkyard is my life. I loathe the stomach-churning idea he would send me off to be married to some Prince. I don't want to get married, never have. Never will.

"However," Matriarch Xenobia says more to herself than to Mister Ed, "now is not the time to be picky. With the historic merger, I'll take whatever scraps I can get. *You*, Windy, let us be off to the Palace. Come now."

"Puff, NO!" I growl to the Matriarch's utter, slack-jawed disbelief.

"Seize her!"

I'm racing to my room in the next instant. Iron-clad feet storm behind me, a hiccup after, heavy and deadly. Mister Ed screams for them, the Keepers, not to hurt me. Not to harm a hair on my head.

My home is no longer safe. My home is infested with Keepers, who will manhandle and beat me like a punching bag. To carve holes in my wings. To steal me away from this Junkyard haven I've known as my home. My sanctuary, where Keepers are forbidden to enter.

Were forbidden…

As fear snakes through my veins and my chest tightens with anxiety, a rush of adrenaline clambers—no, roars!—up my spine. It is then I decided what to do next.

Fight back!

Chapter 3: Windy

My bedroom is filled with all the arsenal I'll need to protect myself. Well, sort of. I don't have a giant sword like the Keepers do, nor their protective gear, but they don't have the weaponry I do. That's for sure. Okay, so maybe I shouldn't call it *"weaponry,"* but more like unfinished-projects-that-I-was-totally-going-to-finish... Eventually. Most of what I have to use in my defense are operable gizmos that may or may not need new batteries. Or a good whack with my monkey wrench to get going.

Slamming my bedroom door behind Puff-Puff and me, I crank the green lever beside the door. There are four levers, each color-coded to remind me of their use. Each one was installed to keep me safe from danger. When I was ten years old, I created these safeguards after years of nightmares I didn't imagine would come true. Mister Ed had always said I was safe in my new home, far from the grip of the Keepers. *"But should you ever feel uneasy or think you could use a little more reassurance, we can build some contraptions together. Me and you."* With his help and three years of arduous work and after finding the right tools, we crafted unique gadgetry that would thwart any threat to my safety.

And now, I am about to find out if any of it works. Mister Ed was the guinea pig when it came time to evaluate our creations. Let's just say he had to sleep in a bathtub full of Ms. Madeline's green goop for a few months because he was hurting something bad.

The lever stiffens as a thick, pink sheet of bubble gum unrolls from the doorframe. Just in time, as a Keepers foot bursts through the wooden door. Releasing the lever, I leap over my unmade bed as Puff-Puff rolls underneath it to retrieve my bag-o-tricks. With a huff and a puff, my little Dragon drags my tattered, baby-sized, leafy-green knapsack by his teeth and pulls it to my feet. Hurriedly, I unzip the bag and smile at the machine waiting inside.

The last bastion.

I gasp as a silver fist punches the door, inches away from being trapped by the gum-shield. I point a trembling finger at my collection of Fairy Dolls in the corner of my room. Their plastic bodies twisted at odd angles, legs snapped in half, bodies severed in two, some half-melted globs of wax. They were test dummies for my many experiments gone wrong.

"Off with their heads!"

Puff-Puff waddles over to the dolls and rips off their heads one by one, storing each under his furry, pink tongue. Rolling to my side, Puff-Puff opens his mouth wide, exposing the collection of severed heads.

"Good boy." I smile, flinching as a pair of hands tears the door off its hinges. Lifting my favorite Dragon in my arms, I hold him steady, ready to fire. "On my mark!"

The Keepers stare confusedly at the tacky gum, unsure what they're looking at. The Matriarch screams her annoyance behind them. At her shrieking, one Keeper waves his hand, motioning for his comrades to give him a wide berth. Unsheathing their sword, the Keeper swings at my shield. The sheet of gum absorbs the first strike and snaps back into place. But where the sword had landed, my shield sags a bit to the left.

"Ready…" I breathe against the back of Puff-Puff's head, arms gripped tight around his belly. The Keeper strikes the gum repeatedly until all elasticity is lost, and the gum-shield hangs limp. With a last swing, my shields are down. The Keeper charges into my room, iron fingers outstretched. His comrades follow close behind when I kick a switch behind me. Several wooden barrels, full to bursting with rocks, drop from a chute in the ceiling and crash down on the cluster of Keepers invading my domain. Rocks spill from the barrels, creating a jagged pathway the remaining Keepers must traverse.

When they do, though, I fire away.

Pumping Puff-Puff's round gut, I eject the dolls' heads in rapid-fire succession. Each head explodes in glittering rainbow glory, blinding the Keepers as they are met with a hail of decapitated plastic heads. The Keepers stumble about, swiping left and right, seeking me in through the storm of shimmering aluminum.

"Nice job, Puff-Puff." I kiss him atop his horned head.

My celebration is cut short as a Keeper grips my arm through the glittering mist. Fear floods through me as his hand tightens around my wrist. Puff-Puff blows hot air at them—he's all out of doll-ammo, but we're not out of options yet.

"Activate B.R.A.V.O," I yelp, trying to yank my wrist away.

Whirring and digitized beeping fill the room with clamorous sound. The Keeper looks down near my feet, at the jittering, metallic box, with flickering red and yellow light bulbs, in the shape of a smiley face. In the center of this bot, a metal panel-like maw yawns open as it powers up, its surface showing hints of frost and ice. B.R.A.V.O's poorly carved mouth-hole breathes a frosted breath, cooling the air around me. Then, my robo-friend springs upward, robotic, steel legs unfolding, creaking beneath it as it stands.

The Keeper snorts. "What's that thing supposed to do?"

B.R.A.V.O's lights blink, reds and yellows flashing their final warning. B.R.A.V.O, better known as Brave and Righteous Android, Victorious Outcome (the name is a work in progress), has passed countless trials wherein its encapsulated small rocks and fruits in freezing ice crystals, sure to cause frostbite. The last time I used it was... oh, hells-bells, I don't remember. It was a while ago, but I have faith in B.R.A.V.O!

Go, B.R.A.V.O!

B.R.A.V.O judders, its clunky rectangle head falls forward, and its flashing lights dim. What the Puff was that!

The Keeper snickers. "Let's go, brat—"

B.R.A.V.O explodes.

An ice-cold wave of water erupts from B.R.A.V.O, and I'm sent rocketing out of the window behind me, thrown through the glass and up, up into the sun-filled sky. Mid-flight, I expand my wings, seeking to right myself, my falling body. Unfortunately, I never learned how to fly. Still, my Fairy nature takes over whenever I find myself free-falling from a shelf too high or a Junkyard heap as monstrous as a Great Dragon. Or having a Keeper-fueled nightmare I can't escape from.

Staggering about in the air like a fly struck by lightning, I whip around in dizzying circles, wings flapping. I loop upside down, then come crashing down on my knees, scraping them raw on a patch of gravel. Jumping to my feet, I race through the Junkyard, searching for Tinker's resting spot.

"Tinker," I say, breathless from this event. I need her to get me the Puff out of here. The Junkyard isn't safe. It's overrun by Keepers. And Mister Ed... I frown at the thought of his old face. How could he do this to me? How could he offer me as a garland for some stupid Prince? I've shared my heart's desire with Mister Ed about my love for the Junkyard and how I'd do anything to have this home forever and ever.

Now I'll be a fugitive, possibly banished for what I did to those Keepers, for how I royally disrespected Matriarch Xenobia.

Oh well! I shrug.

I cut through an archway of junk, welded together by the forever-sun biting my skin as it rapidly dries my clothes. Fairies of Zepyteria must be cautious of the forever sun because, although it's a beautiful star of golden warmth, it can also be a deadly ball of extreme heat. Before Quill revoked the moon from Zepyteria, the elder Fairies all agreed life was much easier in this Realm. Farmer Fairies could tend to their crops without the threat of imminent death four hours into their work. It is why food supplies have been consistently low in Zepyteria. The most common foods to eat are cabbages, carrots, and radishes because of how low maintenance those veggies are. Eventually, you grow sick of the same old same every single day.

There's a clattering behind me. And I dare not spin

around to face my tormentors as the heavy footfall of the Keeper's steel-clad feet, the rustle of their armored bodies grows ever closer.

"Tinker!" I shout, twisting my head left and right. She's not resting under the darkness of the shade where I last saw her. "Oh, no," I cry. I think Tinker flew away to Goddess-knows-where. Why doesn't that Dragonfly sit still? Tinker is always rushing to go somewhere and only comes by when she needs food. Welp, that's the last time I'll give her any morsel of sustenance.

Worse than Tinker leaving without saying goodbye, I'm stuck at this dead end, fenced in by wave after wave of insurmountable junk. Sure, I could climb the heaps of scraps and metal, but I'm winded and near the point of passing out. This is too much excitement for one day.

The Keepers surround me, closing in on me like a pack of lionesses do their prey. I grab the nearest thing to me to help combat these creepers—a titanium tube—Tinker's leg; it must've slipped off. I swing my weapon wildly, like a mad Fairy with their back against a wall. The Keepers mind their distance, keeping away from the Fairy with a titanium death tube in her grip.

"Move aside." Matriarch Xenobia shoves aside the Keepers, who protest the monarch, afraid she might be on the receiving end of my rage. I swing at her, overwhelmed by everything happening around me. Matriarch Xenobia, quicker than the eye, yanks the leg out of my hand, and I tumble forward into her. The Matriarch stares down her button nose at me, her face twitching with restrained ire. "That's enough out of you. I'm annoyed, covered in filth, yet very intrigued by your curious creations. You'll make a fine garland for the Prince of Quill." She wheels me around, her hands firm on my shoulder.

The Matriarch glides as if walking on nothing but air, graceful and fluid, while I trip clumsily over my tired feet beside her. "Edward," she says as we round back to my home, where Mister Ed dares not meet my eyes, burning wild with resentment.

Mister Ed is standing in the doorway, leaning his full weight against his shillelagh. "I-I'm so sorry, Matri—"

"Edward," the Matriarch says through her teeth, "had I known I'd break a sweat in this Junkyard, I would've dressed for the occasion." Matriarch Xenobia squeezes my shoulder tighter, nails pricking my skin. "Say your farewells, Windy. We'll be off to the Palace toot sweet!"

I have nothing to say to Mister Ed. He betrayed me in the worst way possible without my consent. Had the old codger talked to me, I would've laughed in his wrinkled face and thought it was a joke because I'd never—and have never—opened my yap to gush about being a Prince's garland. That's an impossible reality that will never happen...

Shouldn't happen.

Will happen...?

Mister Ed gulps and extends a shaky hand to me. "Windy..."

What I say next are words geared to break Mister Ed's heart like a sledgehammer to the soul. "I hate you."

Chapter 4: Nigel Cloud

"Prince Nigel," Tyeese, Father's caretaker, summons me via my bubble-com on my wrist. Her sorrowful voice, weighted heavily with the daunting task of caring for the King of Quill, shudders a ripple through the bubble. "Please come to King Nigel's chambers as soon as you can. It's urgent."

I mutter a curse beneath my breath, incensed at all I will inherit if Father passes. When he passes, that is. The Kingdom of Quill had seen better days thirty years ago when Father and half of his court devoted their blood, sweat, and tears to building an Aqueduct that would serve the four Fairy realms: Quill, Crest, Abethia, and Luxon. The Aqueduct would supply freshly recycled water, cleansed daily by a magical gemstone the size of a fully grown tree. The stone was split evenly into four pieces by Father's bone-crushing sword and gifted as an offering of peace to the other Fairy realms. All except Zepyteria, naturally.

"I'm on my way," I say into my com, a tired sigh escaping me. When I look about, vision cloudy with sweat blinding my eyes, the cavern I'm in sparkles with starlight spilling in from tiny pinpricks between the golden brown sediment. "Come, Mikah, we must make haste." Mikah and I travel to the Aqueduct almost daily to investigate the crime scene with the hopes of discovering something that could lead us to the culprit: a strand of hair, a footprint, a scale from a fairy wing. All our efforts are for naught, sadly. We'd also hope that, maybe, a fragment of the gemstone was, somehow, left behind. Then, we could start small, hoping to restore the water to Quill. Little by little.

Unfortunately, we've had no such luck.

Mikah Prue, my best bud since birth, stands knee-deep in

thick brown sludge, hands on his hips as he nods. That mass of muck was once refreshed water two months ago, freely flowing from the Kingdom to the townsfolk. It wasn't until a week after a servant noticed brown flecks in our drinking water Father came to investigate. What he saw—well, didn't see—brought him to his knees.

The cleansing crystal had vanished without a trace.

Mikah grabs hold of my hand as I pull him from the gully. Inspecting his stained brown trousers, he asks, "Should I change? Or do you think I can pull this off? Perhaps Tyeese will want to give me a sponge bath like she does King Nigel?"

I shouldn't laugh, but a small snort escapes me. A feeling of something awful gnaws at my spirit because of the sheer immensity of this drought. The rightfully apoplectic townsfolk. And Father's sickness: wither—something akin to dehydration, but far worse that comes with drinking tainted water.

"Come on, then, Nigel." Mikah swipes his hand down one pant leg. With his pointer finger, he dabs the tip of my nose with muck. "Let's stay positive." He lifts my chin and blinks his brown eyes at me.

"Right. Right." I straighten my back, wipe my nose with my sleeve, and loosen my tight shoulders. With one hand on my dagger, for comfort reasons solely, I list my head and beam at my friend. "You have something. Right... there." I gesture to his pristine blond hair that mimics tiny knives.

"Where?" He wipes a muck-devoured hand through his hair.

I erupt into a belly-aching laugh. Mikah's hair is slathered in the nastiness; the tiny spikes glued down in a heap of brown.

Mikah frowns at me for a split second before we both snigger despite the state of the Realm around us. I'm going to miss *this* when it is my time to claim the throne from Father.

That day might be today.

The stars, glimmering brightly against the infinite mauve sky, encircles the gorgeous, heavenly white moon: full and round and marvelous. That floating rock, imbued with ceaseless light, has worked overtime day and night for nearly thirty years. The Zepyterians are to blame for this. Not that I don't enjoy the moon, and its cold. However, I've heard tales from Father the sun —bright, warm, and inviting—is the most splendid creation the Gods could've bestowed upon the Fairy realms.

It's the sole reason I've agreed to... to join in union with the Zepyterians. It's my last resort to revive Quill, restore my Realm with fresh water, and reclaim the sun for all to experience.

"Have you told your Father yet?" Mikah unhooks a flask from his tattered leather belt and imbibes whatever potion is within. "About your agreement with Matriarch Xenobia?"

I refuse his offered drink when he shakes his flask at me and say, "No, I have not. I want it to be a surprise when, in his coming last days, he can marvel in the sunlight. And possibly feel the rain against his skin." Mikah and I traverse up the star-infused quartz stairwell that trails to the star-shaped entryway to the Kingdom. It's a long and exhausting climb and very painful at times when my legs beg for a respite from a day spent investigating high and low. But I must keep my strength about me. I'll be King soon; no time for chicken thighs.

"You're going to marry a Fairy from Zepyteria. That alone is why I drink. My liver will thank you for this, Nigel!" Mikah playfully gives me a shove, his hand imprinting brown on my white vestment, embodied with a star emblem over my heart. "Maybe you shouldn't tell him," he says. "It'd probably be the final blow to his mortality."

Green eyes meeting his brown eyes, I frown. "That's my biggest fear."

Father dying in any capacity is my biggest fear. But watching the slow, decaying effects of wither steal the light from his once healthy body is a torturous event. I'd rather he go in a heated battle with Ogres than this. I wish there was a cure for his ailment. There isn't one because wither is an unknown phenomenon that has all the Healers across the four realms in a tizzy as they collaborate to find a cure.

It might be too late, though.

"What's this?" Mikah's eyes dart from me to the crowd of townsfolk converging in the kingdom's foyer as we climb the last step. It's not uncommon to have the townsfolk gathered in my Father's home. Most gatherings are in celebration of cherished Holydays or Father's birthday. Some townsfolk have enjoyed extended stays in the Kingdom, finding rest and relaxation in the comfort of luxury.

However, this... this gathering is different. Strange. Unnerving.

"Starry morrow, Quillians." I bow with proper gentlemanliness, one foot before the other, one hand against my drumming heart. Instead of returning the gesture—as commoners should—they collectively glower at me.

A townsfolk—I think her name starts with a "G" or possibly a "Z"—flashes her teeth at me, her chartreuse wings buffeting my black hair. "How could you!" She waggles a rose gold envelope in her hands.

"How could I what?" I inquire, brows lifted. This was not the reply she, nor anyone for that matter, desired to hear. And they let it be known: a firestorm of maddened voices coalesces into infernal chaos. The townsfolk, foaming at their mouths, each pinching a curious envelope in their hands, encircle me. An icy shiver rushes through me as I try to find the words to calm them, to douse this growing wildfire.

"This is not how I want to die," Mikah says behind me.

"Enough!" Comes an all too familiar voice that brings an abrupt end to the commotion. Every townsfolk drops to their knees, heads bowed, wings spread wide in a sea of stunning colors. My father, King Nigel Cloud II, looks down upon his court from the balustrade above the imperial staircase. Father is in his nightgown, a ruby coat bejeweled at the collar and chest with star-shaped gems. At his side, holding him by the arm to stabilize his body, Tyeese shakes her head at me disappointedly. Father should be resting his bones to reclaim whatever he can of his former self. Revealing his withering face, sallow complexion, and decaying wings, losing their magical splendor is enough to shatter my statuesque composure. I know it pains him to show himself to his court in such a state, but here he is, dying right before our very eyes.

"Nigel..." His tone is soft but carries an edge that verifies my suspicion. He knows. Of course, he knows. Father is a brilliant Fairy. Nothing gets past him.

"I'm sorry, Father," I blurt out, wringing my hands. "I... I only wanted the suffering to end—"

"By inviting Zepyterians to Quill?" a townsperson shouts.

Then another follows, "They're soulless Fairies, void of feelings."

"You'll never make as great of a King as your father."

"Shame on you, Prince Nigel."

Although their words sting, I mustn't allow them to move me to anger. Anger is an emotion Father has never displayed before his court. His tone is always soft, caressing, and gentle.

"You all should have more respect for Prince Nigel," Mikah snarls, popping his knuckles as if he's soon to engage in a fisticuff bout with all the townsfolk. I've seen my best bud in a few brawls, and let's just say, he enjoys scrapping with any Fairy who regards him in an askance manner.

"Please, let us be calm." There it is, that soft voice of his that could force the most ferocious of Dragons to surrender. Father's command over his court is something I don't think I'll ever have. The townsfolk acquiesce, although some still mutter their disapproval of me. "My son," he says, "I love you enough to give you the benefit of the doubt. Still, as it stands, Zepyterians are our—" He wets his lips, seeking the right words. "—they aren't companions we should associate with."

Father, guided by Tyeese's strong but gentle hands, descends the stairs. His movements are slow and painful. Each step, every breath, takes a toll on him. We're all silent, holding our breaths, watching with misty eyes as my beloved Father—the King of Quill—struggles to remain upright.

"Right here is fine." He smiles at his caretaker. He's

halted on the landing, twenty steps away from his court. "My apologies." Bowing his head, he continues, "I wish I could shake the hands of all the Fairies who've come to voice their concerns. Unfortunately, I am too..." he huffs wearily. "This wither has eaten away my strength, and I wish it gone from my body every day. When my life ends and my body turns to stardust, my son, Nigel, will become your new King. I ask that you all give him a chance to speak. Perhaps... perhaps he has his reasoning for inviting the Zepyterians to Quill."

Father stares at me and waits for me to break the awkward silence. The townsfolk have all focused their eyes on me as well. Nothing left to do but tell them the truth.

Shaking off my nerves, I ask one of the townsfolk to provide me with the letter they received. Mikah plucks an envelope from a glaring Fairy, who growls like a tiny canine at me. Letter in hand, I tear open the envelope and remove a small, glitter-covered, pink card. The card is written in a curlicued, elegant hand.

I read the card's contents aloud. *"Forever sunshine, Quillian.*

You are cordially invited to the dinner party of the millennium hosted by Matriarch Xenobia, ruler of Zepyteria, and Prince Nigel Cloud III of Quill. We'll have games, fabulous prizes, and Prince Nigel shall be wed after desert to a Zepyterian Fairy of his choosing.

See you all tomorrow at first-star shine.
May the waters bless you.
—The Palace of Zepyteria."

"Well," I start, swallowing thickly, sweat beads on my brow. Every Fairy is listening intently, a parade of wide eyes pinning me to the spot. Their pointed ears swiveled my way to catch every word I speak. The most important Fairy, the one I only care about, stares down his nose at me, patiently awaiting what I will say next.

"Father," I say, exhaling slowly, "I did this for you." Father frowns at me. I hurriedly add, "My last wish for you is to revel in the sunrise as it ascends into the heavens before you..." I dare not finish that; instead, I remind him of the moment when he told me he missed feeling the sun kiss his skin. Whatever that means. "We were in Mother's garden when..." Closing my eyes, I relive every moment I've ever had with Mother. Moments that cannot be replicated. When I open my eyes to behold Father, he's standing before me. Father's wings, beating gingerly, whirling with artic blues and lily whites, expand half the foyer's length. The townsfolk gathered around, reach up and graze their fingers on his scales, whispering prayers to the Gods for Father's benefit.

"Remember that day?" I ask, smiling up at him, and he nods knowingly. "You and Mother danced in the garden, and you told her her wings had the sun inside them."

Father lays a hand on my shoulder, and my legs wobble. "Yes, my son. I also recall how upset you were after. Do you remember what you said that day?" He ruffles my black hair; a single brow lifts questioningly.

I sigh playfully, and together we say, "I don't want a brother!" We laugh—his laugh a gentle chuckle, followed by a few concerning coughs. Mine is more like a happy sob.

My legs wobble again, creaking beneath me, then there's a cracking noise. My eyes widen as Father realizes what's happening. But it's too late. Father's reflexes have been dulled due to wither. I come crashing down, my legs spilling from under me and twisting in a gnarly manner as wooden splinters poke through my pant legs. There's a scream. And another. The townsfolk back away from me as if I had become a monster.

"Look away! Look away, will you!" Mikah is on the job, shooing every Fairy away from me. But they know the truth now. It's written on their faces, the disapproving shakes of their heads. Every Fairy in Quill will know my secret, one I've kept hidden for over nineteen years with the help of Mother, Father, our staff, and Mikah.

Father's wings enclose around me, shielding me from the spectators, yet their whispers are loud and clear. Their Prince—soon to be King—is imperfect. Defective.

Chapter 5: Nigel Cloud

I loathe that sensation of helplessness, of vulnerability, of weakness. Of being seen as a defenseless Prince. I'll be the talk of the Realm forever and ever until the day all the Realms in existence wink out like the stars that have burned so brightly in the ether. I want nothing more than to prove I am a Fairy who is more than capable of taking care of himself and supporting my needs. And the needs of all the Fairies of Quill, whatever they may be.

But for now, as I am wheeled helplessly in this maglev wheelchair, I can do nothing for my future constituents but mope. Yes, I could fly, but flying through Father's Kingdom will tire even the youngest of Fairies. I must sit and wait until Davidson, the Realm's most cherished carver, is finished crafting two sets of spare legs for me. Davidson has been the one to help keep my secret for years, never missing a growth spurt, a birthday, or bi-monthly prosthetic maintenance.

Mikah sits cross-legged in the grass, surrounded by cosmos flowers basking in the starlight. Although he wears a worried expression, he seems to relax as he bites down on a fluffy apple muffin. "Ah, so delicious!" He offers me a bite. I refuse, and he shrugs. "More for me then."

"You shouldn't eat too many of those," I say, watching him lick his fingers dry. "Sugar poisoning is widespread amongst Fairies in our age group." Glancing about the spectacular garden Mother so loved, I frown. I wish she were here to wrap her arms around me, to tell me everything will be okay. That I'm making the right choice by marrying a Zepyterian Fairy. It's the only way I can restore a sliver of Father's former self. He'll see the sun, beam with joy, and think of Mother during his last days.

"Do you think I'm foolish?" I ask Mikah, now lying on his backside with his hands clasped behind his head, his eyes darting back and forth as he gazes upon the twinkling star showers.

"Yup!"

"All I want is for Father to be happy."

"I know. I know," he says, "but I can't help but get the jitters—something ."

I growl, "Don't you dare jinx this special occasion to come."

"Special Occasion!" Mikah shoots up to his feet, displeased. His hands are balled as if he is prepared to swing at me. I flinch in my chair, shutting my eyes, ready for his knuckles to sting my cheek. It wouldn't be the first time Mikah and I have fought… and I could bet my legs, if I had any right now, that it won't be the last.

Instead of taking his anger out on me, Mikah storms to the Grandfather tree with its gnarled roots, thick trunk, and decaying leaves. He punches the tree once, twice, ten times before he stops, panting. He's an impulsive Fairy with untreated anger issues. But I dare not tell him that at this very moment.

"I can't protect you from *her*!" Mikah thumps his head against the tree.

"Her?" I question, squinting, head tilted. "You mean Matriarch Xenobia, don't you?" With just a thought, I glide forward in my wheelchair to my best friend. "Is that what has you so upset?"

"Of course, it is!" He gives the Grandfather tree a few more wallops, chipping away splinters. "I don't hit things for no reason, do I?" Yes… Yes, you do, Mikah. It is what's landed you in hot water plenty of times.

"No, you don't," I lie, saving face.

"If I am to be Commander of the Quillian Knights, I must do whatever it takes to protect my King." I promised my best friend the highest honor of becoming the Commander of the Quillian Knights when I was much younger and lacked foresight. Mikah would be a disastrous Chief. He's yet to lead with his brain and not his emotions. Now's not the time to mention this revelation to him.

Nodding with understanding, I admit, "I appreciate all you've done for me. You've protected me since we were both in diapers. You scrapped with fellow Fairies who dared speak ill of Father or me. You've even kept my darkest secrets… until it was revealed by my negligence." I pat my thighs, swaddled in a blanket.

"It was my fault." Mikah kneels before me, bowing his head. "We should've wrapped up our investigation in the Aqueduct hours ago. All that strain on your body must've caused you so much pain."

I've grown used to the pain of having false limbs. However, I will never grow accustomed to Mikah placing the blame on himself. "I'm the one to blame," I say in his defense. "Searching the Aqueducts every day provides us with nothing but a headache. Yet I drag you along, hoping we'll uncover something."

Mikah lifts his head, lips twisted. "We're close to discovering something, Nigel."

"It's what we may find that bothers me so."

"What do you think it could be?"

"Ogres," I say bitterly.

Mikah shakes his head in disagreement. "Ogres have an aversion to water," he deadpans. "It's why their kind smell like manure. It must be a Fairy—one of those herculean types. We should investigate all those muscle-head Fairies—"

"Investigate?" Father's voice makes me jump. Mikah prostrates himself before my wheelchair. "What are we investigating?" He drifts around my chair, his wings a slow, melodic beat.

"You should be resting, Father!" I ready myself to stand when, at the last moment, I remembered my legs were being repaired. I collide with Mikah, who stands as I fall.

"Nigel!" Mikah guides me back to the safety of my hovering chair. "Are you hurt?"

"I... I can't feel my legs." I snicker. Mikah punches my arm; I yelp my hurt, all the while laughing.

Father clears his throat. "Please amuse me with whatever you two were conversing about." He descends onto the lush grass, body jittering from wither.

Tyeese shouts from behind. "King Nigel..." she says breathlessly. "I was preparing a bath when you vanished from your bed. Thank the Gods, I've found you. I quite enjoy having my head attached to my shoulders. Thank you very much."

"I'm quite all right, Tyeese." Father waves his caretaker away, cross with having Tyeese glued to his side like a leech—a helpful leech, that is. Father and I are alike in that we love our independence and hate being seen as the dependent type. Yet, Father needs all the help he can get. "Now, what were you boys talking about? Some investigation? Care to fill me in?"

"You needn't worry, Father," I say, twiddling my thumbs, restless in this seated position. "Mikah and I were discussing the missing cleansing crystal. Sharing ideas on whodunit is all."

Father's eyes flick to Tyeese hovering near my chair. "You're dismissed for tonight, Tyeese. I would like to have a word with my son and Mikah, please."

"B-But, my King..." Tyeese scratches at her neck, distressed by her early dismissal.

"Go, enjoy the rest of this starry night." Father smiles at her, to which Tyeese bows deeply. "Please enjoy some extra cupcakes on my behalf."

"Yes, my King."

We're quiet, Mikah, Father, and I, until the beat of Tyeese's wings falls away on a passing breeze. The star shower above, sparking and fizzing with heavenly colors, lighting the dark sky asunder, ebbs to a dwindling ember.

Father follows my gaze. "Cherish it now, my son," he says cryptically. It's unlike him to speak in such a low, ghastly manner. Despite his illness, Father has always kept a smile on his face. Now, though, the Fairy standing before me, with a deep frown aimed at me, is an unfamiliar Fairy.

"What were you investigating? Tell me now?" Father's jaw tightens.

"It's nothing, Father—" Father waves a hand dismissively at me, then turns to Mikah, shivering in his boots.

"M-My King." Mikah has his head bowed. "Nigel and I were merely t-talking about the missing cleansing stone. W-We we're going to—or rather, had the notion to—investigate potential suspects." My best friend crumbles to the ground, face deep in the grass. "I'm sorry; please forgive me."

Father regards me with a glare so withering I shrink in my chair. I'm a little Fairy again, being punished for something Father forbade me from doing... and yet, disobeying his demands has always been second nature to me. Father restricted me, and Mikah, from entering the Aqueduct because of the ongoing investigation. Father had been adamant he would resolve this matter, but his sickness had earned him more days of bed rest than out hunting down the culprit. He's had no time to sleuth about the Realm, so I took matters into my own capable hands.

Pressing through the shame I feel, I straighten my posture. "I was close to cracking the case, Father. You can punish me however you see fit, but I think I'm on to something."

Father's frown wobbles. Something unusual, foreign flashing across his features. He retains his focus on the starry realm, with millions of celestial bodies confined in his domain. Father, gazing heavenward, confesses something most shocking. "I've known for two months who the culprit was."

Mikah rips his head from the grass, his perplexed expression like mine. Mikah and I exchange bemused looks, our minds in sync, addled by Father's affirmation.

"Why didn't you tell me?" My voice, an unfamiliar roar, startles the three of us. I hadn't meant to speak to Father like that. I've never hazarded a try, either. "How could you keep this from me?"

"It was to protect you!" Father inhales a sharp breath.

"Protect me from what?"

"I thought I had *it* under control," he rambles, "I sent my best Knights away to seek him... my brother. Those Knights never returned."

Brother? What in the stars is Father talking about? Perhaps the wither is getting the best of Father; maybe he's a touch delirious. Father was the only Fairy born to my grandparents, and I his only son.

"Father," I say desperately, "we must get you to bed. You're not making sense."

Father stares at me, his eyes wild. "My son, there is a secret about the Fairy Realms that, upon your coronation, will be illuminated for you. It seems as if my brother will pay us a visit. And thus, all things in the dark must come to light. What impeccable timing my brother has."

"F-Father, I don't follow..."

Father wheels around, his wings unfurl, beautiful under the starlight. Whirling with color, Father's wings flicker with faint images of a tale long ago, impressed upon the moving portrait on his backside.

"What do you see, my son?" he asks over his shoulder as I squint.

My attempts to follow the moving pattern make my head swim. "I-I'm sorry, Father, I don't understand—" I pause, lean in closer to the artwork dancing on his gliders, buffeting the grassy field. The shape of hunched beasts wielding clubs and hammers makes me gulp. "O-Ogres?"

"Yes, my son," he says, "the Ogres are coming."

Chapter 6: Leopoldo

"Cursed reptilian brain!"

The spell Stepmother has enchanted young Leopoldo with was and is the bane of his existence, the thorn entwining his ever-thudding heart. It's the club that batters his immortal soul to be ensnared under her hex. But it was *his* choice! A Dragonborn like Leopoldo, with such a rebellious soul, uproarious nature, and mouthy disposition, sealed his own fate.

He had challenged his wicked stepmother with a chest puffed with vainglorious bravado that it cost him everything. His Pa, Lucious the Cunning, thought it'd be an excellent test of his son's will to survive, to thrive under the direst of circumstances.

"You must find a girl who possesses pure Dragon's fire within her essence," Lucious said, the grin on his face unsettling. It's as if he wanted his youngest to fail, to stay trapped by his Stepmother's hex. "Leonitus Jr. the Jewel, and Leon the Magnet, have already bested their little brother in courting a myriad of Dragonesses. Your brothers are favored in Azolla and worshiped like the gods they will soon become. And then there's *you*..."

Lucious' seemingly never-ending spiel about Leopoldo's failures as his son had turned the Dragon's once jovial heart to stone. The constant comparisons to his brothers Leonitus and Leon had only hardened his resolve to prove his Pa and Stepmother wrong.

"Darling," Leopoldo's Stepmother, Erakna the Marvelous, interjected, drained from the inconvenience this day had grown into. "Should Leopoldo fail his quest, he'll be banished like that whore who birthed him. Oh, and lest I forget, trapped forever as a—"

"I accept the terms of this spell, Stepmother," Leopoldo snarled, baring his canines. Stepmother rubbed him the wrong way since the day his Pa announced to the entire realm he was to remarry days after his Mother's... betrayal and subsequent banishment. He has yet to forgive his Pa for this arrangement. "I'll prove the both of you wrong! I will find the most wondrous bride in all of Azolla who will accept me—curse an all."

Pa and Stepmother chuckled, their glamorous scaled armor clanking as their bodies convulsed. What was the meaning of this? Why were they laughing at Leopoldo? He had no doubts they thought of him as the incapable wyrm of the bunch, but their chorus of laughter was something else...

"What are you not telling me?" he had asked.

It was too late then. The spell had snaked its wispy claws around Leopoldo's throat, clouded his vision, and hissed sweet nothings in his ears. Stepmother's voice bellowed loud and clear: "Your Father has this extraordinary idea to send you to... well, you'll soon find out. What I can tell you is your brothers will be there to have a little fun of their own as well. Leonitus and Leon have an unyielding desire to slaughter the one responsible for your mother's banishment."

His Pa's insidious words came next, but they became garbled as Leopoldo's mind shrank, and words lost meaning. "Heart... Devour... FEAST!"

Blackness swallowed him whole. He was weightless for mere seconds until he was viciously slammed into a new world. And a new body.

And then... then he saw her...

Windy.

Chapter 7: Windy

I hate you!

I... I said those words to Mister Ed, right to his face. I told the Fairy, who saved me from a life of captivity, a life of agony that haunts me whenever I close my eyes, that I hate him. I wish —oh! I wish!—I could take back my words and the pain that certainly split his heart in two. But... Mister Ed had it coming for being a sneaky old, wrinkle-faced, hunched-back—

UGH!

My breathing spikes, lungs burning as my hands tighten to fists, and I stomp my feet on the crystalline floorboards of the Matriarch's carriage. The Matriarch, opposite me, legs crossed beneath her tulle dress, with her hands delicately planted atop her knee, makes an irritated noise.

"Now, look at what you've done." Pointing her polished finger, she brings my attention to the muddy scuff marks on the transparent crystal. Beyond the stains, Zepyteria, the entire Realm, and its Fairies are as tiny as toy figurines. The forever-sunny Realm isn't too shabby from way up high: crystal towers refract indigos, violets, pinks, and blues across the Realm. When the glowing star is centered just right in the vast blue, Zepyteria is a wonderland of vibrant rainbows.

"Sorry," I grumble, shooting her a glance. The Matriarch's coral-pink eyes send a chill through me. There's an intensity behind those eyes that perhaps results from chasing me around the Junkyard or something else. Whatever it is, I don't want to know.

What I want to know is: "Why me?" I ask, gaping at the procession of flying carriages drawn by powder-white unicorns, where Keepers ride alongside the Matriarch's crystal cart. "Why did he do this?" I meant to say that part to myself.

The Matriarch replies, "Why not?" She shifts the cross of her legs, and, from my peripheral, I can see she's watching me like a hawk does a mouse. "What's wrong with being a garland for such a momentous occasion? This merger will bring about a ripple effect that will bring peace back to the five realms. Are you against peace? Are you against me? Perhaps you have built-up animosity towards what I've had done to you when you were my prisoner?"

There's a certain lilt to her words, a discord that slowly moves my gaze to fall upon the Matriarch. Aside from her beauty, those high cheekbones and flawless skin caked with maquillage, I spy the cracks in her visage. The crow's feet around her eyes, the smile lines on a face unfamiliar with the beauty of a smile. For all the great, the marvelous, the spectacular things the Matriarch has done, she is still as normal of a Fairy as I am. The only difference is her status. Her status gives her the freedom to do as she chooses—good, bad, and ugly. One of the ugliest things she's probably ever done was to have me, a baby, tortured and starved and...

"I was innocent..." A boiling surge of hurt, pain, and venom curls my fingers into fists. My nails bite into my palms as I draw in a ragged breath like a Fairy drowning in an endless, piranha-infested sea. I thought—hoped I had overcome the trauma the Keepers inflicted on me. I've worked hard on burying the past so that my future will be uninhibited by it. Yet, here I am in the presence of the Fairy responsible for everything.

"I'm sorry, Windy." The Matriarch's words don't register to me; they're uncharacteristic of her. Unnatural. Sorry. Sorry isn't enough. Sorry doesn't erase the pain, leaving a blank slate in its wake. I can't accept her apology, so I remain silent, with my nails digging deeper into my palms.

"I did what I thought was right to purge the evil from your body." There it is, her reasoning for allowing her Keepers to torture me. Had I expected anything more from her? This is the same Fairy who denied water rights to the four Fairy Realms in dire need of water. I often wonder how the other Fairies of the Fairy Realms have fared for this long.

Tucking a stray hair behind her ear, Matriarch Xenobia raps her fingers musically on the translucent bench. "Blame your parents for what's happened to you. Had they stayed in Luxon, and asked politely, I would've considered sparing them a drink. Instead of doing such a thing, like the barbarians Luxoners are, they founded a mob and tried to have my head."

I'm not the outspoken Fairy type, nor a backtalker or anything of the sort. I respect my elders. I even respect the one elder I may harbor an intense, um, dislike for because he sent me to be a garland for a Prince. Despite all the aforementioned, I snap at the Matriarch. The ruler of Zepyteria.

"Didn't your parents ever teach you how to share? Or have you always been so selfish?" I clasp a hand over my mouth, afraid of what else may leave my lips—a twinge of something reckless curves the corners of my mouth into a tiny smile behind my hand. Maybe, if I'm hotheaded enough, the Matriarch will ship me back to my home sweet Junkyard.

Matriarch Xenobia's jaw slackens. Not too much, or she'd look clownish. She still holds her poise and decorum while addressing me with steepled fingers beneath her chin. "Windy Breeze," she says my name softly, like a gentle tap on the shoulder, "I'll allow that sort of transgression only once. I mean it. Let me share a tidbit of information about what it means to be the Matriarch of thousands of Fairies who need structure and order. Things Edward failed to teach you in your miserable existence."

Leaning a fraction forward, the Matriarch's tulle dress rustles as she grabs a fistful of her garment. "Do you know how hard I've worked to sustain peace within *my* Realm, girl? Do you know what it takes to be a Matriarch? To be under a microscope since the day you were born? I didn't choose this life; it chose me. I don't expect you to understand an iota of it, you sniveling brat. I wasn't supposed to rule Zepyteria—my brother was! He was the favored, the chosen one. The Fairy everyone adored and..." The Matriarch cuts short her rambling and sits back with a *thunk* of her upper back on the translucent bench. Her facial muscles twitch, cheeks spasming, unsure if they want to lift in happiness or droop in melancholia.

The Matriarch's brother, Prince Maestro Xenobia, is a Fairy I am unfamiliar with. He vanished like a phantom thirty-plus years ago, never to be seen or heard from again. The Prince was well on his way to becoming ruler of Zepyteria. His crowing ceremony was set to happen the day after his sudden disappearance. The ceremony was temporarily halted until a formal investigation had been completed.

The Prince was never found.

Princess Jordana Lynne Xenobia came to power soon thereafter. It was a first in Zepyterian history that a female Fairy held the highest seat in the Realm.

"I follow the path Namanzi had laid for me," the Matriarch says, her voice low, raspy. I twist my lips, confused by this latest revelation. "The Goddess dictates who may have a drink of water. Who may bathe in it. Who may be blessed by it. Consider yourself one of the lucky ones, Windy." She gapes at the horizon with eyes searching for something, her jaw clenched.

I soften my fists and will my venomous tongue, ready to slay the Matriarch with deadly words for her role in my earlier years, to relax. The Matriarch seems so vulnerable, lost, and hopeless right now. Should I ask about her brother? Should I even ask anything at all? I loathe sitting in the quiet, especially when a royal and I share the same space.

And... I was bestowed with the gift of gab, thanks to Mister Ed, when I had first laid eyes on this beautiful Realm. I had to ask Mister Ed about everything: the strange flowers growing by the apothecary, why the female Fairies wore gaudy hoopskirts, why the Junkyard was so stinky. I was a natural blabbermouth.

"*Those are silphium, harvested for their medicinal qualities,*" Mister Ed would answer. "*Hoop skirts are what the wealthy wear to* attract a mate. I find it ostentatious, myself," he chuckled. "You'll get used to it—the smell. I hardly notice it anymore after sixty years. Or... seventy. Eighty? I forget how old I am."

A teensy tiny smile glides the corners of my lips up. Though I'm still upset with the old Fairy, I must admit he's been a staple in my life, always there to answer any ridiculous question of mine. Always there by my side.

I still can't figure out why he'd do this to me? What was his reasoning? So many questions riddle my mind like a madhouse of infinite doors that leads nowhere. It's useless to overthink, to try to find an answer. The only Fairy who can give me an honest answer is Mister Ed. Maybe I'll have a chance to see him before my trip to Quill.

"Matriarch Xenobia..." I begin, the weight of her royal name heavy on my lips, "Is there any chance I may speak to Mister Ed soon? Tomorrow maybe?" I need another day of cooling down and regaining my composure before speaking to Mister Ed. I'd hate for my temper to get the best of me. He deserves an apology—as do I. "And I need to kiss Puff-Puff goodbye as well." I hope my littlest Dragon is doing okay without me. Puff-Puff and Mister Ed don't socialize whatsoever. The old Fairy and balloon Dragon don't get along much, either. Mister Ed has, in more ways than one, shown his dislike for Puff-Puff. He tolerates Puff-Puff at a minimum.

The Matriarch makes a face at me, nose scrunched. "I'd ask what in the Goddess's name a Puff-Puff is, but I'd rather that stay a mystery. Besides that, Windy, I must deny your requests as you — and my choice of garlands for the Prince of Quill—must be aloft come the first sun shower." First sun shower is in less than six and a half hours. The Matriarch is on a tight schedule, I see.

I begin to wonder about getting enough sleep and if I'll have enough time to redye my hair, considering the Palace of Zepyteria is rich with fruits, when a buzzing noise interrupts my thoughts. The sound emanates from the Matriarch. She fishes around her tulle for the source of the chirping. She takes a good while to search through all that fabric. Finally, Matriarch

Xenobia unpockets her light pink crystal-com, refracting the sun's light in my eyes, and answers the call.

"What is it?" She presses a finger to her free ear. I watch the Matriarch's face slip from annoyed to questioning to utterly furious. "What do you mean, lost? Find her, or I will have your head, Charles!—" she clenches her jaw and glares at me as if I am the reason for her perpetual anger. Forcing a smile, the Matriarch shows her teeth, perfect and white. "Windy," she says lightly, "might I entice you with an offer worth your while?"

"What is this offer?" I ask, anchoring my attention on her. "Is the pay good? Because I so want to expand the Junkyard, and Mister Ed hasn't had a job in forever. This could be a good thing. Right?"

"Sure, sure." That wicked smile doesn't leave her face, not even when she says, "How'd you like to become a servant of Namanzi? Instead of the Prince's garland?" I've only been this close and personal with the Matriarch for almost an hour, and I don't believe the uptight Fairy knows how to tell a joke. So, this offer of hers must be legit.

I never wanted to marry a Prince anyway. "Uh, okay."

"Splendid."

"So, can I go back home and—"

"No!"

The Matriarch snaps her crystal-com closed, tucks it away, and continues to smile at me. She appears to have calmed down. Her heavy breathing has slowed to a more natural rhythm. But there's something beneath this smile, something I can't quite put my finger on. It's hard to read the face of a Fairy who's had more facelifts than I've had birthdays.

I guess being a servant of Namanzi is far better than marrying a stupid Prince. Yet, I can't shake this gut feeling I've made a terrible mistake.

Chapter 8: Windy

The Palace of Zepyteria must be—no, is!—the most magnificent, beautiful, awesome-sauce place in all the Fairy realms. Paintings and photos of the Palace are a giant disservice—a smack in the face—that does not truly capture what a fantastic wonderland the Palace is. Golden spires like spears pierce the cerulean sky, spilling fresh rainwater upon my skin and hair. Crystal columns refract colors that leak upon a velvet carpet, reds, violets, and yellows trailing up the Palace stairs. A row of servants on opposing ends of the marble stairs greets the Matriarch and me with bowed heads and broad smiles. Some kiss their fingers in proffering so the Matriarch may keep Zepyteria lush with freshwaters; others fall to their knees, tears riddling their eyes.

The instant the Matriarch and I cross the threshold through an arching pink crystal doorway wide enough to squeeze four and a half mammoths through, we are bombarded with scriveners and cooks, toy makers and florists, tailors, and perfumers.

This is too Puffing much! I didn't know what to expect upon entering the famed Palace, but this is overwhelming. I'm sure Matriarch Xenobia is accustomed to this craze; it must be a daily occurrence. With a quill in hand, the Matriarch signs scrolls and makes quick talk with the toy makers and scriveners. She gives a warm smile to a tailor holding a fanciful gown and waggles her nose curiously over tiny vials the perfumer waves beneath her nose.

This crush of Fairies vying for her attention has me dizzy. My hands judder, shaking wild, my breathing spikes, and my skin prickles with unease. I need to break away from this fiasco and fast. I'm having a panic attack. Nothing new. It comes with years of unhealed trauma. I need to take a few deep breaths and —

A hand grabs me from somewhere in the chaos. I stiffen as I am pulled out of the crush and toward a plump female Fairy, eyeballing my hair, clothes, and shoes. She wears her caramel hair slicked in a neat bun, and her figure is clad in a fitting dandelion-yellow evening dress, winged at the shoulders. "You must be the latest edition to the garlands," she says, grimacing at my muddy boots. "I am Nathania, the Matriarch's cotillion specialist. Had you been admitted with the other girls last month, I'd have had more confidence about the Matriarch's decision. Follow me to the showers, please." Nathania flutters ahead of me; her wing beats fast, impatient.

I scurry behind her, dodging the ever-growing crowd swarming the Matriarch. "Um, wait," I call to Nathania halfway down a hall with portraits of the royal family from days past. "I'm not a garland anymore," I chirp. "The Matriarch and I had a little discussion about it, and she and I both agree it'd be a match made in hell if I were to marry a Prince," I snicker, amused by my silliness.

Nathania doesn't find me too funny.

"Until the Matriarch gives me her word," Nathania says as she opens a gilded door with a crystal knob shaped like a rose, "you'll have a shower because you reek like canine turd. Then you'll have dinner with the other garlands. This way, please."

A waft of hot, steamy air rushes past me, nearly melting my face off. "I've already showered today," I protest Nathania's hands, shoving me into the steamed washroom. "Too much bathing causes your skin to fall off." I read that somewhere in the paper... I think. Besides, I think I smell good enough to eat dinner.

"Well, let's hope your old skin falls away, and you'll simply be washed down the drain." Nathania fans her hand, clearing the thick fog. "It'll be less work for me to teach you proper etiquette. Chin up! Back straight! You have ten minutes to get yourself together. Should I be forced to fetch you myself, it will not be pretty. I'll have a gown... and proper heels waiting for you after you've cleaned yourself. Don't forget to wash behind your ears."

"But... I..."

The washroom door slams closed, leaving me with my thoughts and this insufferable steam. With a groan, I search through the fog for the nearest shower, twist the knobs until the temperature is manageable, disrobe, and hop on in.

With a giggle, I pump my fist in the air, thrilled I am no longer a garland. Yet, I'm not too thrilled about being a servant of Namanzi. I'm not the overly religious type, nor have I ever set foot in a sanctuary. But I bet my life that being a servant of the Water Goddess is better than sharing a miserable life with a Prince.

Chapter 9: Leopoldo

I shall marry Windy Breeze one of these splendid days, the banished wyrm sang in his head, his tongue lapping at wet, brown muck. Muck is a much more delicate word for what the plump Dragon was consuming. *Windy shall be mine forevermore! For my name is Prince Leopoldo... the wyrm.* Leopoldo clung to the vestiges of his true self in a far corner of the teensy brain he was rewarded with. The natural instincts of this form took over—more than took over. It consumed him.

But Leopoldo was strong. Perhaps, not strong enough to resist the alluring aroma of the... muck.

I must rescue Windy from the Palace, but I am so famished that my stomach has rendered me useless. Cursed me.

"Brother!"

The balloon wyrm rolls upright from his resting position in the decadent pool of syrupy slush, cooling his gleaming viridian scales, redolent with a dreamy smell of blissful stink.

Who's there? He blinks at the blazing sun as two shadowy figures descend from an iridescent rift in the sky that collapses to nothingness as the two strangers land beside the Dragon.

"Waddling in mud, I see." That voice was so familiar, and yet Leopoldo's pea-sized brain was too fogged with the gluttonous urge to fill himself with sweets that he couldn't—

"Leonitus," one of the shadows says, "I don't find this amusing. I mean, look at him! He's a pathetic wyrm, festering in his own excrement. I don't find joy in this game Stepmother has arranged."

"Leon, Leon, Leon," Leonitus tsks his displeasure, "we've been tasked with a rewarding game of which both our Pa and

Stepmother hopes we'll see through to the end."

"I understand that," Leon retorts. "I don't find solace in making Leopoldo's life any more miserable than it is right now. Stepmother has no intentions of affording Leopoldo the opportunity to break his curse. Should our littlest brother find the girl with that spark of Dragon's fire inside of her, were to slay her. But that's only if he's fallen for the girl."

"Dear brother." The sassier of the two grins gleefully. "Unlike you, I've been keeping tabs on our littlest brother. And unlike you, all I require to unlock his mind, to investigate if he has found love, is this—" He slides an ovate gemstone on his ring finger, dazzling like the forever sun.

Leon rolls his eyes. "Of course," he says, pinching the bridge of his thin nose, "you are the Jewel of the family. You and your love for all things shiny."

"We are Dragonborn, are we not?" They snicker in unison. "Come here, you."

Leopoldo is scooped up from his muck puddle, screeches his dismay, and extends stubby paws at his former resting place, needing to lick and lick. It's in a Dragon's nature to strike those who offend. However, being reduced to whatever species of Dragon Leopoldo's essence haunted, he wasn't sure if these charming males were his friends or foes. Perchance, they had crumbs of food to offer him? Maybe one of those glowing rings on this male's fingers was to be a snack for him. Leopoldo could only hope.

Leonitus then slid his ring finger to the middle of the Dragon's scaly brow.

Everything—all his memories, hopes, dreams, and adventures in Azolla—come flooding back to him for a split second. Leopoldo remembered these two beings casting their eyes upon him: his brothers.

Then, like a lightbulb with fragile filament, his memories fold in on themselves, collapsing until they were tiny specks, blown away by a strong breath of gale.

W-What's going on? Leopoldo blinked at the two strange

creatures with pointed, scaly ears, curled horns, deep red eyes, and elaborate jewelry around their necks and wrists.

"He *is* in love, brother!" Leonitus exclaims, removing a ring from their finger.

Leopoldo's furry tongue lolled in sweet anticipation. A treat? No. No. Leonitus blew his breath on the stone inset in the middle, fogging the jewel.

"Are you certain?" Leon asks, biting their sharpened nails.

"Her name is Windy. She has blue hair and the most beautiful eyes I long to pluck from her skull."

Windy? My master! The tiny Dragon squeals, drooling at the maw as he recalls the endless supply of treats she's shared with him. Gumdrops, sugar bread, honey peppermints, and chocolate-coated crickets.

"Let us be off then, Leonitus!" Leon says.

"Yes, indeedy!" Leonitus grins and pauses to stare at the door of Windy's home, where Mr. Ed is fussing about the domicile. Leonitus's claws tremble, curling into a ball.

"We'll return to have fun with that homewrecker soon enough!" Leon pats the bejeweled Dragon on his shoulder. "I hate him as much as you do, brother. However, we must pace ourselves. For now, let us see about this Windy character, shall we?"

Suddenly, Leopoldo is dropped like a ball and, with a squish, lands face-first in delicious mud.

Windy. I must... must warn her. Of what, though? I must warn her about how hungry I am. Yes, that's it!

Now... which way to the Palace?

Chapter 10: Windy

"Slouching is for the poor!" Nathania claps her hands; two big drums that explode with noise. "Suck in your gut! Males like their females as skinny as a toothpick."

The tailor has her flat foot against my back, pulling at the strings of this awful corset cocktail dress I must wear to dinner. If she pulls anymore, I may die of asphyxiation. I feel woozy after the dress is secured to my body like a second skin. The tailor takes a moment to catch their breath on a fainting chair in Nathania's chambers and motions for a servant to fetch her a drink.

Someone's being overly dramatic.

"Have a look." Nathania glides a hovering mirror to me. She's all smiles as she relishes in my shock and awe.

"I'm pretty." I turn to the side, ogling my fantastic rear in this wine-red corset swing dress. I then examine my makeup: eyelids smoky black, lashes thick with black mascara. There's rouge on my cheeks, bright red and jarring. My lips are stained with blackberry, adding a depth to them that brings the corners of my mouth to my ears.

"We must hurry." Nathania snaps her fingers at me. "A simple ponytail will do." She glances at my locs and half-smiles. "That color doesn't suit you at all. That shade of blue is all wrong."

"I like it." I gather my locs in one hand, and using one loose loc of my tight curls, I wrap that piece around my assembled hair to create a ponytail. Done and done.

"That'll do," she says. "Now, about those ridiculous boots." She holds a pair of heels by the straps for me to take.

"These will give you height and grant you the gift of femininity. A gift you need to quash this tomboy energy you give off. Do you know what they say about tomboys?"

I ignore her diatribe about me being a tomboy. "My boots stay!" I twirl in my boots, mud and all.

"Fine." Nathania tosses the heels onto her bed. "I'll let the Matriarch deal with you. You're a month too late for me to... reconfigure, but, as you've indicated, you're no longer a garland for reasons I do not care. Maybe Matriarch Xenobia came to her senses and realized that a tomboy and a Prince do not mix. I am curious, however, why the Matriarch needs you in the Palace at all. A girl like you will never fit in with *us*!" Nathania shoos me out of her chambers, down the long stretch of carpeted corridor, and points me toward the dining hall.

If I weren't so starved, I would love to explore the Palace of Zepyteria to uncover all the secrets this big ol' place has hidden. I'm sure Matriarch Xenobia has a secret tunnel she uses to traverse the palace without being accosted when she steps foot outside her chamber door. And I'm almost certain there is a trash heap with goodies lying in wait for me to swipe. I know these uptight-and-fancy folk that dwell in the Palace throw away jewels and gems, obsolete computing devices, and out-of-date fashions I could use for my creations. I can't even begin to imagine all the wonders I could create with trash—no, treasure! —from this Palace. Surely being a servant of Namanzi comes with its perks, right? I've got to talk to the Matriarch about that. After dinner, I must find out where all this royal trash goes.

"...glad to serve you, Matriarch Xenobia," someone says from within the dining hall, which smells ahh-mazing.

My nose picks up sweet and spicy flavors, maybe oven-roasted chicken doused in caramelized brown sugar and honey. As I draw closer, I nearly faint at the buffet displayed before me: turkey stuffed meat pie browned to perfection, buttered mashed potatoes, pearl onions and sweet peas, decadent chocolate cake, Fairy rice pudding, and a bowl of crystal candies. Puff-Puff would die of a sugar overdose if he saw that big bowl of sweets.

I'll snag some candies for him.

"Ahem," someone clears their throat as I make haste to the buffet, ignoring all the onlookers with their eyes trained on me.

"Just give me a moment," I say, a mouthful of buttered bread pinched between my teeth and a plate of food growing into a mountain of everything-I-believe-I-can-eat. "You really know how to chow down, don't you, Matriarch Xenobia? Gosh, this is *the* life! I can get used to this! No more yucky-nasty brussels sprout for me. I'm going to eat like a royal! Puff, YEAH!"

"Excuse me!"

I whirl around, chewing like a mad cow. "Huh? What?" I peer around and suddenly become so-so small.

Every Fairy is gorgeous, dressed to the nines in lace, tulle, leather, or peacock feathers. I am so out of place amongst the Fairies of high society. Every Fairy looks perfect: perfect teeth, perfect shiny hair, perfect posture, perfect... everything. And here I am with a massive serving of food, in a dress way too tight, wearing boots that garner whispers amongst those seated at the banquet table hosting the Matriarch at the apex.

"As I was saying." One of the standing Fairies with jet black hair like a waterfall over her shoulders, with a face so lovely, straightens as she shifts her gaze from me back to the Matriarch. "We are thrilled to be here with you during this momentous occasion. I, for one, am honored to have been considered a top pick as a garland for the Prince of Quill." There's a round of applause at this.

I snicker, though I had hoped that snicker was in my head. It was not.

"Is there a problem, newbie?" the Fairy with the lovely face glowers, her fingers strumming a black hand fan dangling from a silver thread looped around her glittering, opal dress. Assessing me, my clothing, and my generous helping of food, she asks, "Who are you? And why are you here? Servants are forbidden to eat with us." There are a few chortles that fly around the table.

"I'm not a servant, smart-mouth." Girls like her are why

I dropped out of secondary school so early. I can't take the cattiness and the boy-craziness that seems to ensorcell all the girls my age. It's sickening.

"This, my darlings, is Windy Breeze," Matriarch Xenobia introduces me. "She is a last minute addition to the bunch. However, there has been a change of plans regarding her."

"Isn't that *that* weird girl from the Junkyard?" some Fairy whispers a bit too loudly.

"She's too pretty to live in a nasty-slimy Junkyard," another says.

"Oh, my goodness," another Fairy gasps, "it *is* her. Doesn't she, like, eat scrap metal?"

"Forgive me, Matriarch," Miss hoity-toity begins, "if she isn't a garland, then why is she here? Windell lacks—" she tosses her hands about searching for words "—everything that would beguile a Prince."

"It's Windy," I bark.

"At least she has all that junk to keep her company." Some Fairy remarks, causing an uproar of laughter.

"That's enough, girls." Matriarch Xenobia pinches her lips together, snuffing out the ghost of a smile on her lips. "Windy, you may eat with us or retire to your chamber."

"That works for all of us." Miss hoity-toity sniggers.

"Rhyanna," Matriarch Xenobia says, "let us be kind. Windy has had an *interesting* upbringing. We must treat her as we would want others to treat us."

Interesting upbringing? Funny she'd put it that way. "I'd rather eat alone, thank you."

"Oh, and Windy," the Matriarch says as I get ready to flee with my tower of food, "before you depart, I'd like for you to stay a moment for my special announcement." I huff but don't puff and remain standing, tummy grumbling. "Although your title has changed, I'd like you to journey with us to the Realm of Quill."

I am ready to protest at this, but what the Matriarch says next has me ever-so-eager to travel to Quill. "There is a rubbish heap of bubble spheres, jade and agate gems, and droplets of gold—gold you'll require for a new motherboard for that robotic contraption of yours. I don't think the power source of copper you found in your backyard was sufficient to produce whatever desired effect you had hoped for."

I blink at her in disbelief. The refurbished copper wiring I used was faulty, causing B.R.A.V.O to malfunction. Additionally, I hadn't used my robot for much of anything besides, once, as a temporary icebox for my leftover food.

"What?" The Matriarch's brows rise. "Did you think I was a beautiful Fairy with no brains? Why do you think so little of me?"

All responses I'd like to say fall away, and I simply shrug. I'd imagine being a royal isn't easy, nor is it for the dimwitted. So, the Matriarch must be smart. Scary smart!

Clapping her hands together, the Matriarch rises. She pinches a flute of sparkling bubbles between her fingers. "Tomorrow, we leave for Quill." She pauses as a round of applause fills the hall. "One of you lucky girls—maybe even two or three of you—shall become Prince Nigel's betrothed. After the Prince decides which Fairy—or Fairies—to wed, we shall celebrate. Because soon…" She raises her glass as every breath is held. "Zepyteria shall experience the moon and her stars forevermore."

All the Fairies hop up to raise their glasses, a wave of happiness flooding the dining hall. Even I find myself smiling at this breaking news—the moon and stars will be one with the Realm of Zepyteria after so many years. If what the elder Fairies say is true, the moon is a splendid and magnificent creation the Gods could've ever gifted Fairy kind.

***

Escorted safely to my chambers by two Keepers, I step into a room so opulent I walk ever-so-slowly across the fuzzy carpeting to place my food safely on a nightstand near my single bed. I guess not only will I be dining alone, but I'll be bunking alone, too. Fine by me.

Four vast floor-to-ceiling windows, with a fantastic view of desert mesas southwest of the Palace, allow soft sunlight to warm this freezing cold chamber. I guess the central air can't keep the entire Palace sensibly warm. But I'll take the cold instead of the blazing sun drifting along the skyline, soon to vanish behind the Palace. Before the moon was revoked from this Realm, it would swap jobs with the sun, offering a shade of ghostly night while stars buzzed iridescent colors in the darkness. I bet it looks so cool. I'm nearly squealing inside at the coming changes.

Kicking off my shoes, I race to the window to take in the sight of Zepyteria. I am so fortunate to live in such a Realm, although my being here was not *my* choice. Still, it's a wondrous Realm, and I am exactly where I need to be right now—

Tap! Tap! Tap!

There's a rasping at my chamber window, the last of the four to my far right. Thinking it is nothing more than a bird who has lost its way home, I turn to devour my food. But I'm suddenly motionless, like one of those crystal statues throughout the Palace, because a Fairy is on my bed eating MY food. By the looks of this Fairy, I'd say she's lived in the Junkyard with me: her clothes are tattered, her nails chipped and dirty, her face bruised and swollen.

"Don't scream," she says, licking her finger clean of chocolate. "Please."

But I do anyway and scream my lungs out.

Chapter 11: Windy

She pounces on me—the savage Fairy in my chamber—her hands clasp around my mouth, suppressing my cries for help as I fall on my back. I doubt any Fairy can hear me; my chamber is on the western wing of the Palace, a good way away from the hubbub in the foyer and dining hall. I force my knees into the wild Fairy's chest, and she yelps and staggers to stand. I kip-up to my feet and squeeze my hands into balls.

The Fairy's eyes dart from me to my plate of food that'll be cold after I kick her tush. She lunges for the plate—no!—the cutlery. Wielding a rose-gold knife in her right hand, she holds her left palm out like a crossing guard, demanding me to stop.

"I won't hurt you... unless you hurt me." The Fairy gulps and exhales shakily. "I-I'm Amana."

"Windy," I hiss, eyes drawn to slits as I observe her carefully, watching every inhale, every twitch in her muscles. "What are you doing in my room? And why are you so busted up?"

"Long story short," she says, slowly dropping her hands to her sides, "my sister, Lilian, went missing almost fourteen years ago. She was a prisoner of the Palace, charged with theft... all she stole was a few loaves of bread from a dumpster to feed my siblings and me. She was sentenced to six months in prison and thousands of hours of community service. But she never came home after the six months were up—"

"This is sounding a bit too long." I'm keeping my fists high and ready. Should she want to put her hands on me again, or my food. I'm prepared to fight.

"My apologies," Amana says. "As part of Lilian's

punishment, my sister was sent to the Gnobi desert. In one of Lilian's letters, she referenced something about being a servant of Namanzi. It made no sense... until last week when I finally mustered up the courage to infiltrate the Palace. I waited for so long because I was so scared. Scared of the answers I may find. And, boy, did I find a hell of a lot of answers."

Amana points to her face, the bruises and swelling. "Done by those dastardly Keepers. Rightfully so, though. I did break into the Palace. And now, if I don't escape, I'll be sacrificed like my sister was... and others."

"S-Sacrificed?" My guard falls to nothingness; Amana's story is so compelling I give her a wide berth. I lean my weight against the windows, heated with sunlight on its pane. "What do you mean... I'm so lost."

"If I don't escape the Palace, I'll die here. Or at the temple. Either way, I'm not too thrilled about those options." Amana resituates the knife she's been holding back on my plate of still-uneaten food. "I must reveal to the entire realm of Zepyteria that Matriarch Xenobia has sacrificed many Fairies, all in the name of Namanzi."

"W-Why would she do that?" I ask, my stomach twisting into knots of unsatiated hunger and unease.

Amana gasps, fumbles backward, and knocks over my glorious mountain of sustenance. What the puff has her so spooked?

"D-Dragons..."

"Dragons?" Judging by Amana's reaction, I surmise that whatever she sees behind me is not my little balloon baby. My Puff-Puff wouldn't garner such a visceral reaction. Puff-Puff is too cute to cause Amana such distress. So, I wheel around, hoping that, one, I didn't make a terrible mistake by leaving myself exposed, and, two, because Amana's startlement worries me. "This better not be a trick..."

It's not.

Two Dragons are hovering mere inches from the window. I'm confused, shocked, awed, and terrified all in this moment.

For starters, these two Dragons aren't your ordinary ginormous Dragons the legends speak of, capable of swallowing an entire village whole. They're not balloon-shaped like Puff-Puff, either. They're half Dragon, half male, with thick, black horns curling at the sides of their heads and irises swimming in garnet. Their features are a perfect blend of terrifyingly frightening and divinely beautiful. Their wings flutter softly as feathers, seaweed green and gorgeous.

It's as if I am under a spell that has me glued to this spot, gawking at them. My mind runs in circles, trying to figure out how this is possible. Have I gone totally bat-poop crazy? Or is this a dream? Yeah, that's it. It's a dream induced by starvation because this cannot be happening.

One of the Dragons grins at me, and the other glowers as if unimpressed for whatever reason. Then, as quickly as they appeared, the Dragons blink out of existence as if they were never there. Then, something ball-shaped and flying right for me, careens through the sky and hits the window with a splat.

"Puff-Puff?" I shake my head, ridding my mind of the Dragons. Puff-Puff's face leaves a balloon-shaped impression on the glass as I open the window and pull him inside. I squeeze him close to me, and he coos. Kissing his head to rid his pain, I ask, "Are you okay?"

Puff-Puff licks his nose. That means yes.

Smiling, I set him down, and he rolls over to Amana, who I had forgotten was in the room with me.

"You have a pet Dragon—" Amana lightly smacks her cheek. "Don't get distracted," she says to herself, staring at me.

Both our ears swivel to the door as footsteps sound. Those heavy feet and the clanging of armor can only belong to the Keepers. Spooked, Amana trembles, then sprints for the open window, shoves me aside, and peers at the fortress of cedar trees two stories below.

"Don't try to stop me," Amana says through her teeth.

I think twice before trying to grab hold of her, to stop her. All I tell her is the truth. "You'll die." If I know anything about the prisons and what the Keepers do to imprisoned Fairies, I know that Amana's wings are not ready for flight.

The footsteps move closer, and Amana's panic rises. The Keepers will be here any moment. Amana's distress breaks my heart. It's written all over her face: brows pinched, lips pressed tight, and watery eyes near spilling hot tears. This Fairy is roughly five years older than me, and she's lived five lifetimes in her young life. I know *that* feeling all too well, the helplessness, anxiety, and the forthcoming pain to be inflicted. I was there once, and I never want to re-encounter it. But there's nothing I can do for her at this moment. If I help hide her in my chambers, I'll wind up imprisoned once she's discovered.

"What can I do to help?" I hurriedly implore a question with only one potential end.

"There isn't anything you can do for me." Amana straddles the window, and I cringe, hoping beyond hope her wings, however trashed they are, will aid her on her journey.

"There has to be a way... somehow." Why am I lying to this poor Fairy? There isn't a way out of this. The only way out is death.

Amana fishes a yellowed slip of folded paper from her pocket and hands it to me. "Lilian wrote something... interesting in this last letter to me." Amana balances herself on the ledge and spreads her arms wide. "The Matriarch gave birth to an Ogreling half-breed fourteen years ago."

My chamber doors fly open. Puff-Puff curls into himself, rolls like a ball and squeezes under the bed. Keepers storm inside with weapons raised in preparation for battle, which seems excessive. "We heard screaming," one of them says as I turn to glance at them. "What seems to be the problem?"

"I—" Wheeling back to the window, I'm saddened when I don't see Amana. She's gone. Her final words to me left me more dumbfounded than I've ever been in my life. I glance down at the treetops and whimper. Amana didn't make it far... her body is all mangled.

Why did I look down?

A Keeper pokes his head out of the window. "I found the escapee."

"Where?" Another Keeper comes forward.

"Right there." There's morbid laughter that follows. "Who's going to clean that up? Someone must."

I slink away to my bed and curl into a ball. Amana is dead. The letter she handed me is crumpled into a ball in my shaking hand. I tuck the ball under my pillow and lie still. My hunger has subsided, and all that's replaced it is a hollow emptiness. I didn't know Amana, but I, too, have dreamed of days when I'd rather die than be a prisoner any longer.

Amana made the best decision she could think of.

***

I awaken a few hours later, unaware that sleep had lured me into the comfort of darkness, to a servant opening my door. Puff-Puff, nestled beside me, yawns in my face, his breath thick with hints of chocolate. Rolling over, Puff-Puff heads back to sleepy-land. I wish I had his Dragon brain, small and forgetful. I think my life would be much... simpler.

"Matriarch Xenobia is requesting a meeting with you," the servant says, standing at the threshold. "I shall escort you to her quarters when you are ready."

I groggily oblige and lumber after the servant, my eyes blurry and tongue heavy. I have a general idea of what the Matriarch and I will discuss, yet I do not wish to converse with her. Not right now.

Amana's body, tangled in the branches, will never leave me no matter how hard I will it to.

The servant leads the way to a clandestine lift that takes us straight to Matriarch Xenobia's quarters. With a bow of their head, the servant waits by the open door where the Matriarch rests lavishly in a fainting chair. Legs crossed, chin high, the Matriarch wears a lavender sleeping gown, reading some sort of manuscript.

Entering the heavily decorated quarters of antique treasures collected from each Fairy realm: moon fragments native to Quill, tornadoes encapsulated in bottles from Crest, Abethian silver and gold flowers, and glass containers of dried fruit one can harvest in Luxon. The sun of Zepyteria overlooks these collections, the brightest star in the Fairy realms.

Matriarch Xenobia's collection must have been passed down from generation to generation because there is no other way to explain this assortment of treasures. I am curious how the five Realms lived in harmony before. What were those Fairies like? What songs did they sing? What foods did they eat?

The simple thought of food has my stomach rumbling.

Matriarch Xenobia snaps shut the manuscript she had been reading at the sound of my grumbling tummy.

"Sorry," I say, standing awkwardly at the entrance. "I haven't eaten a thing."

Matriarch Xenobia pats the space beside her, swinging her legs off the fainting chair. "Let us talk." She snaps her fingers at the servant. "Imani, please have something delivered to my chambers for Windy to eat."

Imani bows before vanishing inside the lift.

"Are you all right, Windy?" Matriarch Xenobia tilts her head searching my weary features.

I fold my hands atop my legs. Staring at the polished crystal floor, mirroring my weary face, I bob my head. "I'm-I'm okay."

"Tell me what happened," she demands. "I must know what that criminal said to you."

What should I tell the Matriarch? That Amana has accused her of sacrificing Fairies for reasons unknown. That Amana made wild claims the Matriarch, who is one hundred percent Fairy, gave birth to an Ogre? Or that there are Dragon-men in Zepyteria? Where do I even begin?

"We haven't much time before we must journey to Quill." The Matriarch leans comfortably on the head of the chair, fingers interlaced. "I ask that you not waste my time and hurry this along. I do not intend to be crass. However, I must claim whatever sleep I can before I am to meet the King and Prince of

Quill—"

"She's dead," is all I muster from my lips. My heart picks up speed, thumping in my ears. "Amana is dead."

Matriarch Xenobia makes a noise in her throat. "Hmm, so you and Amana had a chat, it seems."

I screw my face questioningly when I bite down on my lip hard. I said her name, didn't I? Crud... Now there's nothing I can do but tell the truth. And that, that I do so well and haphazardly. What erupts from my mouth is nonsensical as I repeat everything Amana has said. The Matriarch doesn't flinch, budge, or move a muscle as my long-winded story ends. If she were offended by anything I said, or if any of it were true, Matriarch Xenobia shows no inkling that it is or isn't.

One thing I've omitted entirely, though, is the letter Amana gave me. Whether it's my intuition or sheer craziness, something inside of me wants to uncover what I can for myself.

The truth is out there, and it may be stranger than fiction.

"Windy," Matriarch Xenobia starts after an eternity of silence, "I can assure you that everything Amana said is all a fabrication."

"How can I be so sure?" I shift around to assess the ruler of Zepyteria, who remains as poised as if she weren't accused of horrific atrocities against Fairy kind.

The Matriarch weighs my words, wets her lips, and says, "Your distrust for me is deeper than I can imagine. It is not every day I make time for any and every Fairy, Windy. But you are special because... because... I care about you."

I roll my eyes. "You care about me? Well, if that isn't a load of turd." Heat zips through my veins at the confidence with which she spoke. I snort. "No offense, but I get this overwhelming feeling that you only care about yourself." I scan her quarters and add, "And your prized possessions."

"How wrong you are." Matriarch Xenobia suddenly jolts upright. I'm startled by her unexpected movements, thinking she has lost it. But she calms herself, inhaling and exhaling slowly. She plucks a book from her crystal bookshelf and opens it to a seemingly random page. "Here..." She hands me an envelope tucked between the pages. "Read it."

Why does every Fairy want me to read their personal letters?

I do as told, carefully opening the envelopes and unfolding the paper inside. I study the letter, eyes drinking in each word. It's a certificate of adoption—mine. I'm thrown for a loop, tears prickling my eyes.

"Hereby, it is written," I read aloud, "that Windy Breeze, female, three years of age, has been formally adopted by: Madeline Breeze and Jordana Lynne Xenobia." I'm stunned into disbelieving silence. This isn't real. It can't be. Wiping my eyes, I question the authenticity of this certificate. "What is this?"

Matriarch Xenobia blinks away water fringing her lids. "Madeline and I were lovers, to be secretly wed nearly twenty years ago."

"W-What?" My eyes must be as big as the crystal globes atop the Matriarch's escritoire.

"We kept our relationship a secret from our families, but my father uncovered the truth." She chuckles lightheartedly. "Father thought it suspicious that Madeline would tend to my room when I was in good health. As our healer, Madeline tended to the entire court until that day Father caught us..." She squints at me and muses, "You can fill in the blank."

Continuing, the Matriarch jumps ahead to the point when I come into the picture. "Madeline and I always daydreamed about having a family. And then... well, your parents were captured after they failed at overthrowing me." Matriarch Xenobia observes me as if she expects me to react to this. When I don't give her the desired response, she says, "When you were born, Madeline requested she adopt you at once. Unfortunately, adoption laws in Zepyteria are strict: a married hetero couple may only adopt a child."

At this, I scratch my chin. "But you're the Ruler of Zepyteria. You could've changed that law—"

"It's not *that* simple, Windy." Matriarch Xenobia doesn't

elaborate on what *that* is, and I don't pressure her. The Matriarch finishes, "Madeline found some sap—Edward—to marry her in an attempt to adopt you. Furious, I... I kept her from doing so. But, when Namanzi called me to her temple in the Gnobi desert, I knew that no other but Madeline would escort my band and me, ensuring we'd stay on our toes. As a thank you, I allowed her to adopt you. I had two adoption certificates made: one for Madeline and Edward, the other for her and me."

I scratch at the hollow of my neck, thinking. I want to ask her why it took six years for Mister Ed to take me home. I want to ask why didn't she adopt me? Take me in? Provide me with the same fabulous life she's living?

The silence is weighted with my unasked questions.

Matriarch Xenobia reseats herself beside me and places her hand on my shoulder. "Please, share with me your thoughts, Windy."

"Um... that I'm technically a Princess... right?" As my brain is fogged with this proclamation, I think of how the Matriarch has favored me all day. During the carriage ride here, she kept her eyes on me, and what I had believed was a trick of the forever sunlight, a smile was pressed on her lips. That wasn't my mind deceiving me. Matriarch Xenobia has even invited me to Quill to rummage about in their junkyard of wonders. I found it odd initially that she'd let me roam about in Quill in their forgotten treasures, but now... now it makes sense.

Matriarch Xenobia pulls me into her bosom, hugging me so tight I think I might faint. But I don't, and I relax into this awkwardly warm embrace.

Chapter 12: Leopoldo

Leopoldo dreams of Windy. She smiles at him and strokes his face, curious about something as they dance. Two heartbeats singing as one. His hands around her waist, her hands searching his masculine features. Leopoldo stands tall, a protective shield before the Fairy of his dreams—the Fairy with the Dragon's fire swirling through her veins. If it weren't for the foggy border at the edges of his vision, the snoozing balloon would think this dream was reality.

Windy glides effortlessly in an immaculate golden sheath dress; it hugs all of her to completion. Leopoldo, never the one for formal wear, is clothed in a simple white button-down and blue jeans.

"Why didn't you save me?" Windy asks, her smile vanishing from her adorable face. She regards the Dragonborn with such ferocity he is nearly shaken awake by her blazing brown eyes.

"Whatever do you mean, love?" The couple swirl around the lounge in Leopoldo's lavish abode high in the clouds above the bustling city of Azolla. "You're here with me, safe and in my arms. I'll never let you go. Never."

Windy, her face warmed by the chandelier candelabra, darkens with a trail of crimson slipping from her hair, down to the tip of her nose. Startled by the blood, Leopoldo wipes his sleeve across her brow.

Windy's eyes roll into the back of her skull, and she screams a heart-wrenching sound that chills the Dragonborn to the bones. It's a cry he's experienced firsthand when Lucious the Cunning beheaded the traitors who knew of his mother's secret affair but kept quiet about it.

Windy's scream burns him down to his core, disintegrating his essence because when she writhes in pain, he realizes he can do nothing for her.

"Save me, Leopoldo."

In an instant, Windy falls from his arms, her body limp. Leopold's body betrays him at the wrong moment. He convulses: muscles aching and bones snapping. Stepmother's curse is still upon him, even in the realm of dreams, stealing away his Dragonborn awareness and squelching it down to that of a dumb canine. Worse, a dumb infantile Dragon.

His abode, opulent and glimmering with the latest in Azollan tech, mutates into a dungeon where he is surrounded by death. Young female Fairies litter the wet, undulating granite, the blood drained from their bodies. Windy is among them, her body sprawled lifelessly in the pile of Fairies.

"Praise Namanzi!" a familiar, sparkling Fairy shouts in a dress as black as death.

With his tiny legs and miniature wings, the Dragon leaps upward and then flies to Windy. Or at least, he tries to. In an instant, he's hurled backward, the dream world around him tilting on its head.

And he awakens.

Leopold's nose twitches at the smell of chocolate. Sugary, sweet, fattening chocolate. Rolling over on the plush bed, he yips, happy he was a good Dragon, and remembered to save some chocolate for later. The balloon beast begins to wonder how much later it is and where Windy has gone off to when his dream, now a spectral illusion leaking out of his mind with each bite of chocolate, comes rushing back.

With a startled yap, Leopoldo darts off the comfortable bed and out of the open window in time to see the procession of unicorn-led crystal carriages take off into the forever-sunny skies.

Stomach growling—a sudden craving for mud-slathered cockroaches overcomes the Dragon. The ever-hungry balloon wyrm's maw salivated. Leopoldo was a slave to this body and couldn't resist the tug of his rumbling stomach that pulled him away from following behind the carriages and toward the Junkyard.

Chapter 13: Windy

"Oh-My-Fae!" Rhyanna, my carriage mate and the thorn in my rear as we sail the infinite blue, passes her crystal-com to her fellow garlands. Melody, Zanthippia, and Charm huddle around Rhyanna's cellular device, giggling and prattling about Prince Nigel. Prince Nigel's three-dimensional miniature form stands with his back to me. I couldn't care less about how "cute" or "yummy"—as Melody said—or "sexy" the spoiled rich Prince is. All I care about is reveling in the stars. I hope they're as magnificent as the elders say they are.

"Prince Nigel is my dream Fairy." Charm twirls her blazing red hair around her finger, wetting her lips as if preparing to kiss the Prince. Charm is quite the charming Fairy; her name suits her well. She's been really sweet to me. That was until Rhyanna whispered something in her ear about me, and Charm has turned... charmless.

"Is it true that your parents were the leaders of the Clepsydra?" Charmed had asked, her strawberry-stained lips withering from a smile to a frown.

I hadn't had the chance to answer when Rhyanna spoke in my stead. "It is totally true. I did some digging on you, Windy. And I was appalled at what I saw." Rhyanna lifted her chin as if she were a victor. There's no prize for being a bully.

"And I did some digging on you?" I retorted though I had done no digging on Rhyanna. I don't care too much about her to even consider the idea. Rhyanna must have too much time on her pretty little hands.

"Oh, really?" Rhyanna subtly ground her teeth, jaw taut. Her fingers pattered uneasily against the hand fan that appears to accompany all her attire. Whatever she thinks I may have on her has struck a nerve. Now, I wished I had done some snooping on Rhyanna Goldenchild.

"I'm much too classy to reveal my secrets," I said and dramatically tossed a lock of hair over my shoulder. "Just know it's ever-so juicy." With that, I moved my attention to the disappearing Realm below.

The carriage ride was intensely quiet for an hour before Rhyanna brought out her crystal-com, a rose-gold, shimmering palm-sized crystal. Thus, leading to a girlish frenzy of squeals and giggles.

"Prince Nigel is so hot! With a capital 'H'". Zanthippia, from what I've seen before we left the Palace of Zepyteria, has her face so far up Rhyanna's butt that she does whatever Rhyanna says. "Those dimples are to die for."

"Eww, Zana-Zany-whatever-the-hell," Rhyanna says, "please wipe your hands before touching my one-of-a-kind, super-duper deluxe crystal-com. Do you know how much my parents paid for this?"

Zanthippia hurriedly wipes her hands on her floral gown, glittering with sunlight. Rhyanna's brows knit tightly together, giving her a funky unibrow. It's like an earthworm has sprouted, wiggling on her forehead.

I snort.

I shouldn't have done that.

Rhyanna's blue eyes find mine, a question ruminating behind them. "Listen, Windy." She sniffs, my name like spoiled milk on her mouth as she twists her lips. "I've about had it with your negativity. It boggles the mind that Matriarch Xenobia would even allow you to join us. So that you may, what was it again? Oh, dumpster dive."

Rhyanna's followers laugh, fingers pressed daintily to their stained lips. "Can you believe it? While we're romancing the Prince of Quill, this *thing* will be bobbing for trash. How ludicrous!"

I am so over Rhyanna. She's a pretentious brat who grew

up with far too much wealth and not enough heart. "Will you shut the puff up already?" I ask—no, demand! Fairies like her are why I keep to myself and don't have many friends besides Mister Ed and Puff-Puff. I tried to make friends when I attended school, but once every Fairy saw my wings, I was treated as if I had the cooties. An incurable batch of cooties. Then the bullying happened, then my panic attacks intensified. Then I dropped out.

It was the best decision ever.

"Such foul language from such an average Fairy." Rhyanna rakes a hand through her jet-black tresses. "You don't belong with *us*! You never will."

"I'm cool with that." Rhyanna cannot break me, nor will I allow her to think she can. "Just to let you know." I smile devilishly, leaning closer and showing her my fists, "I like to fight. Unless you want a ring around your eye, I'd suggest you shut your yap." My scarred knuckles, from milling through junk, do the trick as Rhyanna's honeyed pallor pales.

I'm not the violent type at all. Yet, I must admit I am enjoying this triumphant feeling vibrating through me. Rhyanna ignores me as if I've faded into obscurity and talks amongst herself and the other Fairies.

I lean my head back, a grin on my face.

With the garlands' attention elsewhere, I pull out the slip of wrinkled paper Amana gave to me in her last moments. Lilian's handwriting is legible in the beginning as she details her journey through the Gnobi desert. There's also a mention of the Matriarch's pregnancy, which the Matriarch—or my secret mother—had said were all lies.

Lilian's writing is rushed near the end of the letter, as if the last sentences had been added as an afterthought. It's as if she cannot express everything happening around her calmly and orderly.

"*Dear sister,*

We've finally arrived in the Gnobi desert, but it seems we are lost. I swear the Matriarch's caravan has circled the same formation of rocks over thirty times. Speaking of the Matriarch…

I have some shocking news to relay to you! It's about the Matriarch herself.

She's pregnant!

Can you believe it? I had never thought the Matriarch of all Fairies to have a child out of wedlock.

How scandalous!

Thanks to some rumbling between the other servants, I found out the Matriarch was expecting. I wonder who the Father is… we can use this to our advantage if we can find the bastard. I can only imagine the money we could make off of this. No more stolen bread for us; we'll eat like royalty.

Until my next letter, give everyone a kiss for me. I miss you all." The letter initially ended here, with Lilian printing her signature halfway on the parchment.

Then the letter takes a turn for the strange as Lilian's writing is rushed and nearly unreadable. *"Her lover is an Ogre. I can't believe it… but… everything I've seen so far in this temple hints that Ogres are an integral part of Nasturtium."* Lilian's letter is illegible for the next few words. *"—Fairies. Dead. Sacrificed."* I can't imagine what Lilian was experiencing at the temple of the Water Goddess Namanzi. Still, it seems as if it's too excessive to be believable. *"Servants of Namanzi"* and *"killed,"* and finally, *"Matriarch… Healer… knows… everythi…"* The word Healer gives pause.

Madeline.

Could this be true? Did Madeline know about this?

If I think on it long enough and given what Matriarch Xenobia revealed to me hours ago, then it's best to assume that Madeline knew everything. They were lovers to be wed. Madeline and the Matriarch *knew* each other far too well and too intimately for this not to be true. Who exactly was Madeline Breeze?

The mother I never knew…

***

I can't believe what I see as I awaken from my little cat nap.

For the first time in my life, I am gazing upon a starry realm of wonders with my very own eyes. The moon is full, aglow with a blueish-white light; an iridescent corona encompasses the floating beauty, making it pop against the vast black sky. I must remind myself to breathe as a faint, dizzy spell swims around my head from lack of oxygen.

The garlands are as awe-shocked as I am. Rhyanna and the other snap photos with their crystal-coms, souring the mood as bursts of light flick from their devices. I'm trying to map out the stars, to link hidden shapes of drinking gourds, bows and arrows, and big and little bears, but the blinding com flashes make that impossible.

Soon enough, I'll enjoy this moment on my lonesome while scavenging the Quillian Junkyard for—

"It's the Kingdom of Quill!" Rhyanna startles me with her annoying voice, shoving me out of the way as she and her cohorts scramble to view the starlit Kingdom ahead. "I'll transform the west wing into a study. And, Oh-My-Fae, look how lavish that garden is. Unfortunately, that garden will be uprooted, and a summer home for my parents will be erected right over those fields of roses. I have so many plans for my future as Princess."

Charm chimes in, "I actually like the garden." Rhyanna's neck nearly snaps in half as she glares at Charm. "We don't have pretty flowers like this back home. If Prince Nigel chooses me, I'll try my hand at gardening—"

"And I hope you fail." Rhyanna is not my cup of tea at all. "Let's get one thing straight: Prince Nigel *will* choose me, and do you know why?"

Melody and Charm shake their heads; it's Zanthippia who answers. "Because you're ever-so beautiful and smart."

"Precisely." Rhyanna pats herself on the back. "Genetics and smarts will win out against you three. In addition, I have wealthy parents. I took eighteen years of etiquette classes, and my educational background is spectacular. Neither you, Zan-whatever, or you Melondee, nor you Charma, will ever have the privilege of being on my level. I am a Goldenchild! I dwell in the upper echelon with the likes of Matriarch Xenobia. That, in and of itself, qualifies me as Princess material."

Zanthippia, Melody, and Charm bow their heads, ashamed and near tears. I must remind myself that this is not my fight, that I am not involved. But I can't sit by and watch Rhyanna in silence while she destroys their confidence.

"Silence in the face of evil is evil itself."

"Rhyanna," I growl, posture stiffening as I plant my feet firm, "you're not *that* pretty." Who am I kidding? She's drop-dead gorgeous. "I doubt the stupid Prince would even look your way twice." Turning away from Rhyanna's flaming red face, I address the others. "Don't let her talk to you like that. You are all beautiful and smart in your own special way. Rhyanna is nothing but a bully. And that makes her so-so-soooo ugly on the inside."

Zanthippia, Melody, and Charm give me shaky smiles, their gazes flitting from me to Rhyanna. They're unsure how to respond or whether they should speak up for themselves. There's nothing more I can say that will break them free of their worst fear: Rhyanna. Why are they afraid of her so? I'm confident if they stick up for themselves and throw back the rubbish Rhyanna slung at them to break their spirits, Rhyanna will crumble under their combined power.

Before any of the other garlands can agree—or object—Rhyanna snickers. "Need I remind you three," she says, black-stained fingernails tapping away on her crystal-com, "I have dirt on all of you."

"So, what if you do?" I point my finger at her, swishing it like a lethal weapon. "Need I remind you I have dirt on you, too?"

I don't, but I'm keeping my expression stony, and hard to keep up this façade.

"You know," Rhyanna says, licking her lips, "you had me convinced there earlier when you claimed to have something on me. Silly of me to think that a trash Fairy like you could coexist in spaces where I am basically a quasi-Princess. So, Windy, what do you have on me? If anything."

I gulp as my throat goes dry. If I stay silent too long, she'll know I'm lying and have no ammunition to use against her. The other garlands regard me with weary expressions as they realize I cannot possibly have anything against her.

I fold, throwing up my hands. "You're right. I have nothing on you." I bow out gracefully and reseat myself.

"Like I thought," Rhyanna titters. "You're nothing but trash, Windy Breeze, and you'll always be trash. Am I right, girls?"

Zanthippia, Melody, and Charm all echo Rhyanna's gross statement. "You're trash, Windy!"

Chapter 14: Nigel

"The Zepyterians are coming!" Mikah shouts, dashing around my chambers like a crazed Fairy who has stuffed their face with far too many apple muffins. "The Zepyterians are coming. Hide your younglings!" Amused with himself, Mikah feigns choking, tongue wagging, hands clasped around his neck. "T-They're going to k-kill us all." And then, to add to the drama, he faints. "And scene. How was that, Nigel?"

I scold him with a glare through the full-length mirror I am standing before.

Lola, my stylist, gives Mikah a giggle and a round of applause. "You should've become an actor, Mikah." Lola tucks a stray hair of her grape-dyed hair behind her ear, red tinges her cheeks. Like every female Fairy in Quill, she has a thing for Mikah. "Give us a twirl, why don't you, Prince Nigel."

I twirl to my left and right in my one-of-a-kind custom-made star suit. It's all ivory-white, a blend of silk and cotton that fits just right. A cluster of five-point stars twinkle on the lapels and line the shoulder and cuffs. My ankle-length pant legs sparkle heavenly beneath the moonlit sky swarmed with stars.

"Curiously," Lola says, surveying my chamber for an extra pair of fancy shoes, "it seems as if your feet grew a few inches overnight. So, the shoes I had thought would fit you—" She points to the box of pristine loafers. "—are much too small. I am saddened, my Prince. I did not mean to fail you on such a momentous occasion. I am deserving of any punishment you may have for me." Lola bows her head, trembling.

Lifting my stylist's chin, I smirk. "Lola, you've done an amazing job on such short notice. You'll be paid triple for your trouble. As for the shoes, I'll borrow a pair from Father."

"But... I swore I had the size right."

"No worries." I give her shoulder a good wiggle. "Thank you. You may have the rest of the day to yourself. Enjoy the craziness about to ensue." I give a strained chuckle that alarms both Lola and Mikah. "If you'll excuse me."

Father's chambers aren't too far from mine, and I've walked down these baroque halls countless times. I can do it with my eyes closed should I choose. Today, however, is different. As I clench my teeth, trying to fight the pain of my new legs digging into my thighs, splintering with wood chips, I glance across the hall where a wax painting of Mother stares longingly into the distance.

"Are you proud of me, Mother?" I gather my strength and wade to Mother. Gliding my fingers over the glossy portrait, I ask, "Please watch over Quill... Father has made some wild claims. Claims I hope do not fulfill themselves."

Yet, deep down, I have this nasty, bubbling tar-like feeling that something is about to go terribly wrong. But this emotion isn't centered on the flock of potential Zepyterian wives, no. It has more to do with Father, the Uncle I hadn't known about, and Ogres. What connection do my Father and his brother have to Ogres? Why would my newfound Uncle steal Quill's cleansing crystal? And lastly, why is my Uncle collaborating with Ogres? Could he have been cast out of Quill for betraying Fairy kind by aligning himself with Ogres?

I look toward my mother with pleading eyes; however, she can't do much for me but gaze at nothing but the wall adjacent to her. Father is the only Fairy who can answer my burning questions.

Ignoring the pain, I stride to Father's chamber with my shoulders high and chest out. I must uncover whatever he's been hiding from me to ensure that, when the Zepyterians arrive, nothing is out of the ordinary. Should anything go wrong, should Ogres suddenly appear, this day will go from bad to horrifying.

"Father, it is me," I announce as I open his chamber door.

Father's room is bare except for his bed and regal robes hanging from hooks. Everything that could've potentially been a hazard to Father, who would collapse at any given moment when he was first afflicted with wither, has been removed from his chambers. He's racked up several concussions during the first two weeks of his illness. We had thought he'd lost part of his motor abilities because of his age. How I wish that were the case.

"Yes, my son?" Father stands with his back to me, focused on the incoming fleet of airborne carriages far in the distance through the floor-to-ceiling window.

"Are those unicorns?" I ask, joining Father at his side, squinting. "It's been years since I've seen a unicorn." Unicorns are far more fascinating than the mules we have at the stables. A memory of Mother bubbles in my mind on my next breath, illuminating the faintest of memories of where unicorns surrounded me in a field.

Father fills in the blanks, his intuition far beyond anything I can understand. "Emlyn. She bred unicorns once. I think about the first time I met her. We were teens when she captured my heart after our first encounter." Father presses his hand against the windowpane, impressing his prints against it. "Before the water dried up and the sun made its perpetual home in Zepyteria, a sun shower had fallen over Quill. It was the most fascinating thing I'd ever seen. I had riding lessons that day, long ago, when I met your mother. I was a sodden mess when I arrived at the stables at Emlyn's family ranch.

"I thought it be manly of me to prove to my Father I didn't require any aid—I was to be King soon! Instead of fetching a carriage to the ranch, I walked several miles in the sun shower until my boots were heavy with water. When I arrived, I collapsed from exhaustion, and my body was overwhelmed by a cold. Emlyn cared for me until my cold had passed, and I was back to my old self. I stayed with my future in-laws and my soon-to-be wife for a week before I left."

I appreciate that Father has shared a story I'd never heard

before, yet I did not come here to talk about the past. I need the truth. I part my lips to say so, but Father finishes his story.

"When the water dried up, Emlyn had to set free all her unicorns. It was a sad day for her. For us all. She figured her unicorns were smarter than the average Fairy at finding fresh water to drink. Sure enough, they had: Zepyteria." Father laughs, his lips stretching to his cheeks. "After you were born, one of Emlyn's unicorns returned: Champion. It was as if Champion knew his former master had given birth, and he, too, had traveled with his family to pay Quill a visit. That was nearly eighteen years ago."

"F-Father," I start, raking my hair. "I enjoy when you speak of Mother. However, today... today I'd like to learn more about my Uncle. And the Ogres. And this secret concerning the Fairy Realms. I need answers."

Father retains his focus on the glimmering white unicorns, traversing the starry night, pulling along crystalline carriages, refracting an array of nameless, hypnotic colors. "Emlyn loved you so much, Nigel. She loved you so much... so, so much." Almost imperceptibly, Father's face darkens, brows furrowing, mouth twisting into a snarl. Or was that a smile? Whatever emotion that was, it is erased from Father's face a heartbeat after.

"Father," I say, soft as cotton, tugging at his white cloak too large for his frame. "I ask that you be honest with me, please. Sleep was impossible for me because your confession addled my mind. All I know is I have an Uncle, and he's somehow aligned with Ogres. I need you to fill in the blanks."

"Emlyn." Father is at it again, ignoring my request to babble about Mother. I love Mother, but this is not the time for reminiscing. "She died in my arms."

I squirm at this, thighs shuddering from the newness of my legs. Father has never talked about Mother's demise, no matter how many times I asked about it. *Do I really want to know?* I ask myself. When I shake my head disapprovingly, I try once more to gain answers from Father.

"Tell me, Father. Enough about Mother!" Frustration builds inside of me, a fizzy carbonated drink ready to explode. "What are you hiding from me?"

"King Nigel." Tyeese enters Father's chambers at such an inappropriate time. "Matriarch Xenobia is here several hours earlier than expected. She's requesting an audience with you, my King." Tyeese points her finger at me. "Prince Nigel, Matriarch Xenobia has provided a few garlands for you to interview before the remaining party arrives."

I raise my brow at Tyeese. "I have no time for the garlands; I must accompany Father to this meeting with the Matriarch. Matriarch Xenobia knows I am to be King and has the gall to exclude me from her assembly? Where is she right this very moment? I'd like to have a word with her."

Before Tyeese can muster a response, Father's hand squeezes my wrist. "Matriarch Xenobia and I have history. What she and I discuss will not concern you until *you* are crowned King, Nigel. Until that day," he says and leans into my ear so that only I can hear the hiss in his voice, "I shall take every secret I hold close to my heart to the grave. Including everything about my Brother."

Rising to address Tyeese, Father grins. "Let's be off, shall we?"

I am abruptly left alone with my thoughts and a treacherous knowing that Father is not the Fairy I've always thought him to be.

***

The Kingdom of Quill has a maze of intersecting hallways and clandestine passageways within it. This elaborate labyrinth allows servants or on-duty Knights to find themselves at Father's aid should he need it. Never have I used these halls, hidden behind doorways and portraits of my family, to free myself from my home. I require fresh air, a minute or five to think to myself. Had I waltzed out of the front, I would've been accosted by the garlands in wait. I am not in any apt state to break the ice with small talk about a significant event that is to happen in mere hours.

Starlight dances on my skin, and an incredible rush of wind tingles my face. I've made it outside, unbeknownst to anyone dwelling in the Kingdom. I siphon in the brisk air, filling my lungs to full and gag.

"Stars!" I curse, wrinkling my nose at the tangy miasma invading my senses. Of all the doors I could have opened, I find myself in the one place I've never visited: the midden. Although there are barrels of trash sealed with lids, the smells of everyday life cannot be confined to thousands of wooden crates. These crates are supposed to be shipped monthly to a landfill where everything is incinerated. When I find out who is in charge of removing the detritus, I'll have them docked a year's pay and charged with dereliction.

I pinch the collar of my shirt and delicately cover the tip of my nose with it, careful not to cause a wrinkle. Turning to face the door that sent me to this reeking doom, I try the knob, slick with a layer of pinkish slime. It doesn't budge.

"Great. Just great, I tell you." I stomp my feet, truly maddened by this. I'm trapped; worse, I've left my bubble-com in my chambers. Now, to escape to freedom, I must traverse this stinky tangle of trash—and dare I say, rodents!—to reenter my Kingdom.

Something skitters by my shoeless feet, white and fuzzy, giving my heart a jolt. At least I can't feel my feet squelching atop this foundation of squishy and soft and hard.

A shudder moves through me, from the base of my spine to the tippy top of my head. I steal a quick, shirt-filtered breath into my nose and make a break for the nearest exit way. I had hoped to come to a doorway where discovering one of Mother's secret gardens was a possibility. Or to be rewarded with a spectacular view of Quill from atop the battlement.

But this... this midden embodies the genuine relationship I share with Father. I've always admired him, yes. I love him; indeed, I do. Yet, like the junk-packed barrels stuffed with discarded items that no longer serve a purpose, Father has filled my mind with fluff. The fluffy musings about what it's like to be King of Quill. He's never had a bad day as King. Even with his affliction, he always shone a light on Quill during its darkest hours. But Father has never turned that same light on himself to reveal the truth of who he is. Not to anyone. Not to Mother, I'm sure. And not to the son soon to usurp the throne.

I barely knew of my Grandparent, who were as secretive as Father. I hardly knew Mother, to be honest, aside from the fragmented memories. Then, there's that one memory—perhaps a dream—that never leaves me.

Mother holds me so close to her chest her heart echoes in my head. She's running, running, running away from someone. She says something to me in her haste—a rush of cluttered words that makes no sense.

"It's all lies, Nigel. Everything we believed... is a lie."

Mother screams as someone drives their blade through her chest. She falls, and together we tumble down, down, down. Then Father picks me up, and that's where everything goes hazy.

My vision blurs and fresh tears find their home on my cheeks. I touch my fingers to my chest, tingling with the ghosts of that awful nightmare—

"Watch out!" a female voice warns.

I look for the voice, legs kicking up dirt and rocks, when I suddenly slam full force into a me-sized mountain of obsolete bubble-coms.

The Realm of Quill goes upside down; the stars swirl around my head endlessly. I fall to my buttock and palm my head.

"Are you okay?" That voice again. Their shadow envelopes me, blocking out the moonlight.

Lifting my chin, my eyes land upon the most uniquely beautiful Fairy I've had the pleasure of sharing the midden with. Her body is outlined in a halo of soft, white moonlight. And her hair, like blue ropes, falls over her shoulder as she offers me her hand.

"I'm Windy," she says, taking my calloused hand in her

equally calloused mitts. But there's a softness to them, a magical pulse to them so riveting I don't want to let go.

I blink at her, trying to assess if she is a mirage created by the stink. However, she is far too beautiful to be a mere phantasm. "I'm... I'm..." I reach my fingers to a warm spot on my forehead. "Bleeding. Stars. I'm bleeding."

"Well, Bleeding Stars, nice to meet you!" A laugh escapes her, and it's a hauntingly delicious noise. "Let's get you cleaned up, okay?"

"Yes, please. And thank you."

Looping my arm around her neck, Windy becomes my guide, my lifesaver to deliver me from the bowel of Quill.

Chapter 15: Nigel

"Are you sure?" Windy squints her eyes at me, asking for the umpteenth time if I am certain about my decision. "I'm confident this ritzy Palace has Healers on staff. If not, then you should totally quit your day job. You can't work in a beautiful Junkyard like that and not expect to bump your noggin a few hundred times." She giggles, and I find myself lost in the noise.

I've deduced that Windy is Zepyterian and has come along with Matriarch Xenobia's band for the party slash wedding. I hadn't expected a Zepyterian to be so... attractive. But, as fate would have it, Windy is not a garland. It's evident from her dyed hair, the dirt caked on her dress, to the sack of rubbish she holds over her shoulder. Perhaps Windy here is some sort of spy who rummages through discarded scrap to uncover any secrets that may live within Quill.

But all my theories are tossed into the ether because Windy doesn't even know who I am. Surely a spy for Matriarch Xenobia would know me: the dashing Prince of Quill. Windy doesn't regard me like my fellow Quillians do—with a slight hint of fear and equal parts admiration. Instead, Windy's behavior around me is relaxed.

"I'll be quite all right. I came outside to take a breather. Instead, I've gone and injured myself. Life is funny." I smile while holding my head, wrapped with delicate pink gauze, thanks to my savior with blue hair. Windy has torn her dress to aid me the best way she can. Although the gash in my head throbs and the gauze is damp with blood, the bleeding has been stanched.

Windy's right leg is exposed, unveiling improperly tended scars and bruises on her brown skin. I eye her legs, curious about the markings.

"How'd you get those scars?" I ask, leaning my head against the dilapidated wooden fence partitioning the midden from the evergreen trees along the perimeter of the Kingdom.

I find it most strange there isn't a Knight on patrol on the border where the Kingdom meets the forest. That could explain why Windy is here and has not been apprehended for rummaging through the midden for purposes I still haven't asked her.

"Oh, these?" Windy rotates her leg, assessing her markings as if they were new. "Well, like you, the Junkyard is my home. It comes with the territory—the scrapes and bruises. I have this weird thing about picking my scabs, so my legs look all pockmarked." Standing a few inches taller on her tiptoes, she declares, "These are my battle scars."

There's that laugh once more. Had I been born with an addictive personality, I'd find some way to bottle up her laughter and sell it to all the Realms.

"Are you okay? Really?" Windy's fingers tap my shoulder.

"Yes." I blink my eyes rapidly, lost in the reverie of her. Of Windy. "Yes. I'm all right. Say, did you say the Junkyard was your home?"

Windy bobs her head, thrilled. "It's, like, the best thing ever. I am the luckiest Fairy in all the Realms."

My brows raise. Peering over my shoulder and through a small hole in the fencing, I look at the midden, confused. "What's so special about that?" I jerk my head to one side. "It's nothing but trash," I say, then add, unthinkingly, "which should be burning to a crisp in a landfill. Wait till I tell Father about this."

"You and your Dad work in the Junkyard together?" She's nearly squealing, like a piglet bathing in slop. "My Dad—I usually call him Mister Ed—and I work together in our Junkyard, too. But, unlike yours, ours is not attached to a fancy-schmancy Palace. We have the freedom to work for ourselves. There's no stuffy King to boss us around."

"Stuffy King?" I frown.

"Yeah," she says, "and his stuffy son of a Prince. I'm so happy I am not a garland anymore. All those other girls are pretty much fangirling over Prince Nigel." She says my name as if it's a sour candy, sticking out her tongue. My eyes twitch, annoyed, as she continues, "Like, what's so special about him? Other than he is a Prince? I can pretty much tell you they want the status—the fame! The notoriety! I don't want nor need that—"

I interject, hurt that this lovely Fairy thinks so little of me. "Prince Nigel is a fantastic individual. I'm—he's kind, caring, and wants the best for the Fairies of Quill."

"If he's so kind and caring," Windy bemoans, smacking her teeth, "then why doesn't he provide you with proper shoes? Or better prosthetics? I can whip up something better for you in my Junkyard."

My heart rate spikes, booming in my chest. I glance down at my feet, where my wooden toes poke out of my—once new—now tattered socks. Windy's mesmerizing presence has sucked me into a world where I wasn't different, where everything in the Realms was right.

Windy's brown, star-speckled eyes lock with my green eyes, riddled with fear and anxiety.

"I'm sorry," she says, her tone a gentle susurration. "I should've been more mindful."

I smile at Windy's kind words, and for the briefest of moments, as my gaze falls upon her cheeks, filled with amusement, warmth fills the smile on my face.

Dropping her sack of rubbish-goods, Windy starts, "I didn't mean to make you feel bad about your legs. I know how it is to be different. But different is good, despite what other Fairies may say or think."

Windy shimmies her shoulders, and her wings bloom from her back, blue and black and... frayed with holes.

My jaw goes slack, eyes bulging.

"That's the reaction I usually get." Windy's wings vanish a

beat later.

"I didn't mean to—" I stumble over my words. "I was just... I... what happened?"

Windy kicks at a patch of dirt, her head down. "I was a prisoner of the Zepyteria since before I was born. This, amongst other things, was my punishment."

I voice my concern, fisting my hands. "That's not right. It's unfair on all accounts. Why would Matriarch Xenobia do something like that?"

"Because my parents were water thieves."

I tilt my head, my face quizzical. "Water thieves?"

"Yeah," she murmurs. "My parents were the ringleaders of the Clepsydra. They believed that every Fairy should have access to fresh water. And I totally agree with that, but they went about it the wrong way."

The Clepsydra? That name rings a faint bell in my mind. I'm sure Father knows something about this, among the other things he knows but doesn't care to share with me. Besides that, I'm intrigued by Windy's story.

Perhaps instead of Father's rumbling about Ogres, I wonder if this band of thieves may share some responsibility for the missing cleansing crystal. But, as hard as I try to make it make sense, Father confessed to knowing the true culprits—my Uncle and Ogres.

"So, your family was banished to a Junkyard as punishment?"

"No..." Windy worries her bottom lip with her teeth. "I was adopted. My birth parents paid for their crimes," she says, her lashes aflutter as her head dips.

"I'm sorry to hear that."

"It's okay, I guess." Windy is silent as she wipes her eyes.

"I was born like this." I lift my pant legs to give Windy a better show and shift the conversation from her to me. My legs—more like uncomfortable wooden cylinders with spring-loaded ankles—shudder under my weight. Davidson has lost his oomph in carving; perhaps his age is catching up to him. "I wish

I could say I lost them in war whilst defending my Kingdom, but I cannot. Princes are supposed to be born perfect, not imperfect." I sigh.

I've wished on many a star, prayed to whoever would listen to bless me with *real* legs. All my wishing and praying were for naught. I've been different since birth. One would think I'd be used to my body after eighteen years. That I would've accepted my body as is. Yet, that has not been the case. Not yet, though. I've tried hard, proclaimed self-love affirmations while staring at myself in the mirror, and done all I could think of.

Still, I remain in a constant state of love/hate with myself.

"What do you mean Princes are supposed to be born perfect?" She asks while reassessing me: my face, hair, and stained clothes. Y-You're P-Prince Nigel?" Windy splutters, inching away from me.

I nod shakily. "I-I should've told you. I'm sorry—"

Windy flees from my presence, her hair whipping behind her.

"Wait! Wait!" I call for her.

"PRINCE NIGEL!" Mikah's familiar voice comes from somewhere in the midden.

"Mikah?" I whirl around as the fence door flies open with a crash.

Mikah gives me a once-over. Twice over. Thrice over. "What happened to you!" Mikah unsheathes his dagger. "Were you attacked? Was it—" He lowers his voice to a whisper. "Ogres?"

"No, not at all," I say, turning away from him to the direction Windy ran. "It was a Zepyterian."

"That bonked you in the head?" Mikah bounds in front of me. "Where are they? I knew this was a dangerous plan. They've already launched an attack on the Prince of Quill. Those vile Fairies."

I palm a hand on Mikah's tense shoulders. "Mikah, I got this—" I gesture to the gash on my head "—from not watching where I was running."

"Well, then." Mikah grunts, sheathing his dagger. "You should be more careful."

"There was this Zepyterian here—Windy." Her name births warmth in my cheeks. "She helped me. She was the most beautiful Fairy I've seen with dazzling blue locs of hair."

"Windy?" Mikah cranes his neck around, looking for her. My best friend turns to me and regards my wound with a stiff-lipped grimace before pointing to the sack on the ground. "What's that?"

"Oh, that? It's Windy's?"

Mikah wrinkles his nose. "A so-called *beautiful* Zepyterian named Windy was here with you, Prince Nigel? Collecting Quillian trash?"

"Yes, you've got it."

"I wouldn't put it past a Zepyterian to fester in trash, but to call one of *their* kind beautiful is a stretch of the imagination." Mikah grips my arm and pulls me along. "Come, let's get you to a healer and all cleaned up. You've some mediocre-looking Zepyterians to claim as your forever and always." He snickers.

As we round the fence, I take one more gander at the sack and the dusty trail Windy left behind. I hope to see her again to correct this wrong I've caused. I should've been honest with her and told her who I was. But she has her mind set already when it comes to royalty.

I'd give anything talk to her again. To share our stories.

To forget all that ails me...

Chapter 16: Windy

Why did I run away? Was it because I insulted him and his Father to his face? Is it because I am royally embarrassed by it? Or could it be that I liked him, felt a smidge of giddiness and warmth... Well, yes and yes, and yes to all three. I am mortified by it. Had I known that *that* clumsy Fairy was the Prince himself, I would've never confided in him about my life. I would've never shown him my wings.

I would've left him to fend for himself.

No. No. That's so wrong. I would've helped him. Prince or not. He's still a Fairy with emotions and feelings. And I'm not some heartless, soulless Fairy who'd do something like that.

I've skedaddled far beyond the Palace's estate. Even though it's a ginormous eyesore in the distance with its sparkling spires and battlements adorned with pennons flapping against the breath of night. I've no urge to go back and attend the coming dinner party.

My stomach protests that notion. "Okay," I say, patting my belly. "I'll grab us a bite to eat, but after that, I need to talk to Matriarch Xenobia." It's urgent I do. I can't stay here for... How long are we supposed to be here? I should've asked. In any case, I'll just give her a ring and tell her I want to go home, back to the Junkyard.

Per the norm, thinking of my fabulous Junkyard would usually conjure joyful memories of me dabbling in junk, uncovering extraordinary finds that Fairies disregarded as useless. However, all I can think of is Prince Nigel, finding him in a Junkyard of all places. It's purely a coincidence, right?

I lift my head to the stars, a dazzling sight I can't begin

to describe. Maybe the stars preordained my meeting with the Prince of Quill. Heat kisses my cheeks and coils around my thudding heart. All I can think of is him. It's so strange the first guy to evoke these unfamiliar emotions is him: the stuffy Prince of Quill.

A cackle races from my lips, vibrating my throat. "What the Puff is up with me?" I ask the stars.

Buzz! Buzz!

My crystal-com vibrates in my dress pocket. Mister Ed's face flickers atop the crystal screen as I pull the device out and lay it in my palm. I give myself a few moments of thinking before answering. I haven't spoken to Mister Ed since I declared I hated him. Which, at the time, yeah... I sort of hate him for what he's done. But now... now I need to talk to him. I *must* talk to him.

I have so much to tell him. So much to ask.

I answer the call. "Hey, Mister Ed, how are you?" I ask, half-smiling, still annoyed by my current situation.

"Windy... I hope I'm not calling at a bad time," he says as his holo-image waves at me. "All I wanted to do was check up on you. A big commotion occurred when the Matriarch left the Palace for Quill earlier today. Some Fairies celebrated the occasion with hopeful hearts; others aren't sure about this merger." Mister Ed bends to pick up something, and when he rises, he holds Puff-Puff with one arm. "I think this one misses you."

"Hey, Puff-Puff," I croon, "how's my favorite Dragon?"

Puff-Puff yips delightedly, wiggles out of Mister Ed's arm.

"Your Dragon has been acting strange," Mister Ed says.

I snort and retort with, "Stranger than usual?"

Mister Ed shrugs. "It's as if he can't decide whether to leave the Junkyard or stay with me. Something has him spooked."

"I'm sure everything is all right. Puff-Puff is a peculiar Dragon. You and I know that already."

Searching my surroundings, I stride toward a closed boutique featuring wacky garments in the display window and peer inside. "Quill is... strange. Stranger than Puff-Puff. Here, have a look." I glide my crystal-com from the boutique window to the array of stores surrounding it: apothecaries, pet stores, a tavern, and haberdashery line opposite sides of the starlit, cobblestone road. Not a soul is out; every Fairy must be at the Palace.

"May I see the stars?" Mister Ed asks.

I lift my hand high, giving Mister Ed the best view I can. Mister Ed is silent, and for a minute there, I believe our connection is lost. But his holo extends his hands as if to touch one of the stars.

"Thank you," Mister Ed says gratefully. "It's been so long since I've seen the stars. Please soak up every ounce of this while you can."

"I will." I find myself lost in the infinite glittering splendor. "Um, I wanted to say I was sorry. And I don't hate you. Not even a little. You're the best Dad a Fairy could ask for."

"And you are the best daughter in all the Realms."

"Puff, yeah, I am." I pump my fist, enjoying this moment with the only Father I've ever known. When my hand falls back to my side, I unconsciously tap my fingers against the letter in my pocket.

My reality is skewed once more, twisted by the contents written in it. Twisted like Amana's body upon the treetops.

For the last few hours since I arrived in Quill, I pushed the letter to the back of my mind, wanting to revel in the beauty of Quill. Sooner or later, I knew I'd have to come face-to-face with the realization I'll have more questions that needed to be answered. I wanted to confide in the Matriarch, to ask once more about Amana and if anything the Fairy claimed was true. That would've been a waste of my time, though. I don't think I can trust Matriarch Xenobia in any capacity. Not when Lilian's letter mentions the Matriarch's Healer knows everything.

"Mister Ed," I say timidly, fingers shaking as I grip tight my crystal-com, "I want to know more about Mom—Madeline. I have questions I think only you can answer."

Tapping his chin, Mister Ed replies, "Hmm, I'm uncertain there is anything more I can share about Madeline that you don't already know. Unless you want me to remind you about our almost disastrous wedding again." He shakes his head playfully, cheeks dimpling. "Goodness, was that day stressful as all heck. But it's a day I'd relive forever in a day."

Mister Ed has disclosed his wedding story to me over the years. Whenever he reminisces about it, he says it was the happiest moment of his life. That he'd found his soulmate. Mister Ed, for a time, gave up on love because he doesn't come from a wealthy family. His only inheritance was the Junkyard, passed down from his great-great-great-Grandfather, and so on.

Madeline and Mister Ed had been married a short while before she was summoned to join Matriarch Xenobia to "deliver offerings" to Namanzi. But those offerings were sacrifices...

Amana had said her sister, Lilian, was a servant of Namanzi. A role I gladly took on because being a garland for a Prince was despicable in my eyes. Yet, as I stand here, my mind racing, I realize I've made a grave mistake.

"Are you all right, Windy?" Mister Ed asks, voice lilting with concern. "You've been awfully quiet. Tell me what's on your mind—"

I do, rather harshly, at that. "Was Madeline, like, a pathological liar? Did she keep secrets from you? Did you know she and Matriarch Xenobia were lovers?" I slap a hand over my mouth, hoping I didn't say what I think I just said.

Mister Ed stares at me, forehead wrinkled, as I look down upon him with wide, terrified eyes. My intention is not to hurt Mister Ed, to blind him with scandalous news he wasn't aware of. All I want to do is connect the dots and figure out Lilian's letter.

"H-How did you find out?" Mister Ed plants his com on the kitchen counter and sits atop the barstool. "Did Jordana tell you?" He's calling the Matriarch by her first name; it's heavy on his tongue.

So, Matriarch Xenobia isn't a liar? To some degree...

"Yes..." My tone is soft. "Matriarch Xenobia told me everything. She shared... intimate details about her life with Madeline. And Madeline's true intentions on marrying you—a male Fairy. I'm sorry," I add hurriedly, but Mister Ed waves a hand, dismissing my need to apologize.

"Windy..." Mister Ed's voice is brimming with pain and memories he'd rather forget. "I loved Madeline... and a small part of me believes she loved me too. Yet, it had been glaringly obvious to me—and a few others—that Madeline was swept away by Jordana." I hear Mister Ed's voice crack, the distress and hurt intermingled with the memories he's reliving.

Mister Ed sniffles and prepares himself to shed light on the Fairy I had no sour thoughts about. His mouth opens to speak, but I jump in. "Remember the time I chipped a tooth on that trampoline I found?"

Mister Ed's lips twitch from the frown burying itself on his face to a weak smile. "I recall that moment," he says, shuddering. "You so desperately wanted to fly, despite the condition of your wings. I had warned you, didn't I?" He arches a brow.

I cross my eyes at him and stick out my tongue. "Yeah, yeah," I cluck. "Thank you for being there for me. Thank you for everything. Thank you for—"

"Windy, what has gotten into you?" Mister Ed scratches his chin, affection brightening his white eyes. "I do appreciate your kind words, but it is unneeded. I must be the one thanking you for forgiving me. I shouldn't have done what I did to you—shipping you off to be a garland."

"Why did you, though?" I ask.

"Because I desire for you to find love," he says. "You spend much of your time in the Junkyard and are always by yourself. Windy, you've dedicated your life to working in the Junkyard and never figured out who you are outside of it."

I lick my lips and inhale slowly with the intent of remaining calm. I don't understand Mister Ed's reasoning, and should I speak too soon, our relationship will suffer another blow. I take a quiet moment to align my thoughts, to pick and choose the best response, because if I don't, I will have a meltdown.

"So, you're saying I'm wasting my life away?" Oh, crud! I'm spiraling out of control like a tornado. "That if you didn't send me off to be with a damn Prince, I'd never figure out who I was?"

"You're misinterpreting my words." Mister Ed proffers his hand as if to reach out and take mine. "Don't let your anger get the best of you. Breathe, please. Breathe and understand I only wanted the best for you."

"Maybe it's best I don't come home for a while since I don't know who I am without the Junkyard." My chest tightens as if someone has their arms wrapped around my ribcage.

Breathing becomes difficult for me. I'm a fish out of water, gasping for my life.

"Take a breath, Windy," Mister Ed says from somewhere beyond the dark clouds in my mind, muffling his voice. "You're having a panic attack. It's okay. Just breathe and know I love you so much. You are stronger than this. You are so much stronger! Remember to focus on something that makes you happy and take slow, deep breaths."

I thought I'd overcome these stupid panic attacks. I'd worked hard to rid myself of those nightmares flooded with Keepers beating on me. Worked even harder to accept I was an orphan with no connection to who my family was. It's taken me years to embrace my faulty wings that will never allow me the chance to fly. I've made so many breakthroughs with Mister Ed's help, his guiding hand, that I know what true happiness is.

It's bright and sunny and inviting. And… and… it's filled with love.

I'm slowly returning to reality, blinking away the blurriness from my vision and taking in a huge inhale. In my mind's eye, I imagine myself playing atop a heap of Junk. Mister Ed is there with me in his heavy cloaks, tapping his shillelagh and humming. Prince Nigel is there too, resting beside me, smiling wide, cheeks red from the sun's heat.

Hold on. What the Puff is Prince Nigel doing in my fantasy?

"It's good to have you back," Mister Ed says, his voice snapping me out of my fantasy.

I lift the crystal-com to my eye level. "I'm sorry."

"No need to apologize." Mister Ed rises to stand as knocks pound on the front door. "We're all Fairy here. We're creatures of emotion—I'll call you right back. I love you."

"Love you, too."

Puff-Puff goes haywire in the background, growling and yapping.

"What's gotten into Puff-Puff?" My friendly Dragon isn't the protective type, but whoever is at the door has my littlest Dragon spooked.

The connection drops when Mister Ed ends the call. I'm left standing in the middle of somewhere in Quill by my lonesome. Even though I don't want to, I should head back to the Palace because I am starved! I wonder what food Quillians eat? Whatever they eat, it'd better be good.

I whirl on my heels to face the Palace in the distance and break into a jog. "Hopefully, there's still some food left for me," I say aloud.

This realm is mighty nippy. I've never experienced a cold like this, not even when I had the chills. I wrap my hands around my body, trapping in any warmth I have left when I bump into someone who walks right into my path.

"Sorry," I say quickly as I skirt around the looming Fairy, robed in garments so black they're nearly invisible. The robed Fairy doesn't acknowledge me, so I shrug it off and keep up my pace.

Suddenly, I slow down to a brisk walk. More robed figures are crawling out of the shadows, tall and imposing Fairies who don't give off the best vibes. I'm about a mile from the castle. Its glittering structure is the only light source strong enough to illuminate the surrounding pathway. The stars' light pales in comparison to the glowing Palace of Quill.

The robed figures flank me on all sides, matching my strides. An uneasy feeling grips its claws into my back and forces me to scan my surroundings for a place to run to, for a weapon to use. Had I not left my bag of goodies with the Prince, I'd use it to swing about and knock some sense into these creeps.

"You're an intruder on this land, Fairy!" one of the robe figures hisses at me.

"I'm just visiting." I keep my focus ahead, afraid to look over my shoulder. "I'm here with Matriarch Xenobia!" I shout, hoping to scare them away by mentioning her name. "If I go missing, Quill will be turned upside down. So, you better keep your distance before... before it gets ugly." Okay, Windy, stop with the shenanigans. I can't take on this band of creepers creeping up on me as if I owe them something.

A robed figure blocks me from walking any further. I crunch my knuckles, balling my hands, prepared to fight.

"Tell us what you know about the so-called *Fairy Realms*?" A masculine voice asks, their face obscured by a hood. "What have your educational institutions taught you about Fairy origins? What lies have they planted within the minds of you impressionable young Fairies?"

"Um, to tell you the truth," I say, infusing my words with fiery sass, "I am a teenage dropout. Therefore, I can't tell you a thing about Nasturtium. You're asking the wrong Fairy. Besides, I have somewhere to be. And I am going from hungry to hangry! Move aside. Please."

The hooded Fairy shakes his head at me and then removes his hood. I am lost in a world of chaos, surprise, and horror for a long while. The hooded creeper's face is a startling mix of Fairy and something else. Perfectly pointed ears, familiar green eyes set into a familiar-looking face, and a mossy skin complexion. His most telling feature is the elongated canines jutting from his bottom lip and curving upward.

He's an Ogre!

Chapter 17: Nigel

Mikah stands ramrod straight with his arms folded tight and lips pressed in a thin line. He carefully watches the Healer tending to my wounds, dabbing a damp cloth on my head. The Healer's throat bobs as he steals glances over his shoulder at Mikah, who has been nothing but rude to Pablo since he arrived. Mikah's fear is that Pablo will ask far too many questions, attempting to pry anything about what had happened to me and where I got this bump on my head. The gossip mill in Quill is without slumber. With yesterday's events—where my legs being exposed superseded the news about our soon-to-be Zepyterian visitors!—there have been whispers flitting about I've chosen to ignore.

However, it appears as if that gossip mill hasn't yet reached the tailor. Lola peers at me from the corner of my chambers, afraid to move. Her eyes analyze my semi-exposed legs through my tattered pant legs; worry creases her brows together. Folded in her hands, she carries a "just-in-case" second pair of matching garments to dress in.

"Perhaps you should shower too?" Mikah shoos the Healer away and inspects my head for any faults. "Looks good. Now, be off, Pablo. And don't you dare say a word to anyone."

Pablo bows his bald head to me and scurries out of my chambers.

Lola clears her throat, gingerly shuffles forward, and plants the clothes beside me on my canopy bed. Her eyes are focused on the gilded walls, too afraid to meet mine.

"It's all right, Lola," I say gently. "The entire court knows about... *this*. I'm surprised you haven't heard anything about it."

Lola relaxes her stiffened shoulders. "I... I didn't mean to stare. I-I was only curious—"

"About how I lost my legs?"

"I don't mean to be rude. But, yes, my Prince," Lola says.

Mikah smirks at her. I can tell he's about to create some fable by that wicked lift of his lips alone. "Well, I'm not one to toot my own horn." He Puffs his chest, and I flop backward onto my bed, already exhausted by his tall tale. "But I saved Nigel from —" he lowers his voice, leans close to Lola's ear, "—Ogres. Nigel and I were playing pretend when we were about five or six. I played the role of a hunter, slayer of beasts, procurer of fortune, Fairy of mystery." I groan out my annoyance; Mikah simply continues. "And Nigel was my pipsqueak sidekick. We ventured too far out of the Realm when we were attacked by bloodthirsty Ogres. I had to defend my Prince with all my strength. But those Ogres bested me, and thus... Nigel's legs were torn from his body and devoured by the Ogres. Had I stepped in a moment too late, our dear Prince here would be as good as—"

"Enough, Mikah," I grumble, propping a hand on one side of my face. "I wasn't attacked by Ogres. I was born like this." Imperfect and all. Will I ever learn to accept this faulty body exactly as it is?

Lola speaks through splayed fingers on her mouth. "Ogres?" She breathes. "I had heard through the grapevine—that grapevine being my eldest sister—that Ogres were responsible for stealing our cleansing crystal. Those evil demons are the cause of the drought, aren't they?"

Mikah and I glance at each other, unsure where to go next. On how to spin this story on its head. Father's story about the Uncle I never knew I had, to the threat of *"the Ogres are coming,"* plunges me into a darkness that only Father can shine a light on.

Our silence is enough to widen Lola's eyes in horror and surprise. "Is it true then? Is that why all the Knights are gathered in the Foyer, the dining room, and even the sauna?"

Had it not been for my unsupervised journey through the midden and my chance encounter with Windy, I surmised the Knights of Quill were rewarded with a day of leisure for the festivities. Father must've alerted them to the possible threat of Ogres. Why hadn't he told me this? Does Father believe an attack would occur on the night I am to choose a bride-to-be? If so, every Fairy here is in danger.

I tap my bubble-com, flick through a list of names, then tap Tyeese's name. Her com rings and rings and rings. Puzzled, I look toward Mikah and ask him to do the same. We're both met with the perpetual sound of ringing. Something is wrong. Even if Tyeese were preoccupied with Father, she'd give a quick *"I'm busy, my Prince. I'll give you a ring in a few."* However, her failure to answer is enough to give me chills.

"Are you two all right?" Lola worries her hands together, wringing them.

"Lola." I pause, considering my words before continuing. "Is your entire family in attendance here in the Kingdom?"

Lola starts to weep as if cursed with the gift of clairvoyance. "W-What's happening?"

"Nothing... yet." I hold tight to her wrists, her hands shaking in mine. "Mikah, could you please escort Lola and her family to the Red Rooms. Tell the Knights I gave her permission to be there."

The Red Rooms are reserved for family, and most friends in the event Armageddon rains down on Quill. The rooms are protected by ancient Fairy magic, magic that has not survived long enough to be of any use to the Fairies of today. Magic is something long forgotten with the sands of time.

Mikah steals Lola away from me, calmly presses the palm of his hand to her cheek. "You're in safe hands now." Lola nods her head, tears trickling down her cheeks. "Hopefully, Prince Nigel is overreacting, and everything is a-okay." Mikah gives me an unenthused look, pleading with me not to scare off the Fairy he's trying to woo out of her undergarments. "Call me should anything come up, Nigel!"

The kingdom's halls are quiet, save for the commotion down in the foyer, of which I've yet to make an appearance. I shouldn't be rude to my guests who've come wide and far in celebration. My guests would be appalled if they saw me in my filthy garments with matching dirty hair, but I had no time to change. I've got to find Tyeese. I have this horrible feeling that something has happened to her.

Tyeese last escorted my Father to the roundtable where he and the uncouth Matriarch, who didn't extend her invite to me, are possibly conversing about everything under the moon. Stars only know what secrets they're sharing—royal secrets, that is. Although Tyeese is stuck to my Father like adhesive, she is prohibited from private discussions between royals.

Father's voice swirls in my head. *"There is a secret about the Fairy Realms that, upon your coronation, will be illuminated for you."*

I halt to catch my breath; the restlessness of everything happening around me makes my body weak. I hope I haven't been afflicted with anything from all the ick that surrounded me in the midden. That foul aroma will never leave my nostrils, no matter how hard I try to snort in the perfumed-laden air.

I am nearing Tyeese's room when a giggle-fest erupts down one of the split corridors. A parade of glamorously dressed female Fairies, headed by a housekeep in plain clothes, shows the girls their temporary living quarters. These Fairies are from Zepyteria—amongst the gaggle, one or more of them will be my betrothed. I haven't yet decided if the polygamous route is for me, and I honestly don't think it is. Still, everything I've done up to this point is for the benefit of my Father and all of Quill. Quillians will know the balance of the sun, moon, and stars and

—

"Oh-My-Fae!" one Fairy shouts, her voice echoing through the hall. "IT'S PRINCE NIGEL!" the giggling gaggle of girls stampeded for me, toppling over the housekeep, who crumbles to the carpet in a heap.

"Stars!" I cruse, readying to flee, but I don't because that would be awfully rude of me. Licking my palm, I sweep back my black hair and straighten my spine. "Starry morrow, ladies. I am Prince Nigel Cloud III. It is a pleasure to have you all here." I must say these Fairies are easy on the eyes and the nose. They're of different hues, eye shapes, hair textures, heights, and attractiveness.

I know it's a waste of effort, but I scan the crowd for blue hair and a hint of brown skin. Wishing to see *her* again.

"Pardon me, Prince Nigel." A stunningly beautiful Fairy saunters forward, her walk velvety smooth and seductive in her billowing, black gown. Her hips sway as if she's dancing to an unheard rhythm beyond my comprehension. A fan stung around her hips gives me a slight pause because those things were once used for—

Raising a hand to her cohorts behind her, this Fairy single handily silences the screaming bunch with a wave. This Fairy wields some power over her fellow garlands as if she were a royal. How fascinating.

"I am Rhyanna Goldenchild." Rhyanna bows, her black tresses sweeping over her shoulders. Her deep-sea eyes lull me like a fly to honey when she rises. "It is a great honor to make your acquaintance, Prince Nigel. I speak for every garland here when I say we are thrilled to have this opportunity to unite our Realms. To restore a semblance of peace and hope for all Fairy kind."

I can't help the smile curling on my face nor the heat clambering up my neck to my cheeks. Raising my voice a touch, I announce, "It is my honor to welcome you all to the Kingdom of Quill. I hadn't expected this to turn out as it has because of our respective Realms' history. But I assure you all that my intentions are pure. And filled with the hope of rewriting history, for goodness' sake."

"Prince Nigel," a Fairy in the crowd shouts, "choose me! Please!"

Another cries, "No! Me!"

Then another, "It'll be me!"

The hall descends into chaos, garlands shouting my name, pleading to me with tear-stricken eyes to *"choose"* them, to *"love"* them. To make them a *"Princess."*

It appears like an all-out brawl is about to sprout its nasty head as the garlands push and shove, extending their needy hands to me. Stars, what have I gotten myself into? I hadn't thought this through, hadn't daydreamed this kind of chaos would happen.

Amongst the bevy of clamoring Fairies, Rhyanna whirls to face her fellow Zepyterians, her obsidian ball gown swirling. "Enough!" Rhyanna, with her hands on her hips, huffs, irritated. "How dare you all conduct yourselves in such a fiendish manner? We are guests here in Quill, not savages. As Zepyterians, we must always uphold ourselves with grace and honor. This display before Prince Nigel is highly upsetting to me and—when I see her and tell her what happened—Matriarch Xenobia. The Matriarch will have you all shipped home for such classless behavior."

Wow. I am thoroughly impressed by Rhyanna. How she speaks and demands quiet amongst a throng of Prince-hungry garlands is exciting. Father would be awed by Rhyanna simply because this Fairy is similar in demeanor to my mother. I've heard tales about Mother, how she was a force to be reckoned with, never to be crossed. Mother knew what she wanted and didn't settle for less. That isn't to say Mother wasn't kind or gentle when needed, but the court understood that my mother wasn't to be toyed with.

Rhyanna may be the perfect match for me if Father should have a say. And yet, all I can think of is the Fairy I met in the midden.

Rhyanna turns to me again, the garlands behind her on their best behavior now. She catches my eyes roving the crowd. "Are you well, Nigel?" I meet her curious blue eyes, single brow arched. "Should I call someone to attend to…" she looks me up and down. "I'd hate to be crass, but is this a bad time?"

I tilt my head questioningly. Then I take a gander at my attire and curse myself. I was in such a rush to check in on Tyeese I forgot to change, shower, and cover my legs. I cross one wooden ankle behind the other, catching Rhyanna's attention.

"There's no need to worry, Prince Nigel," Rhyanna says with such scary confidence I take a tiny step back from her. "As we speak, my parents have sought out and talked to the top mechanic in Zepyteria." She retrieves her crystal-com from her dress pocket and summons a display before my eyes.

"What's this?" I squint, lifting a finger to trace the blueprint hovering before me. "Are those... legs? But... how?"

Rhyanna bats her eyelashes at me. "Gossip travels fast here in Quill," she says, much to my chagrin. Of course, it does. "Upon finding out about your situation, I took it upon myself as your future Princess to see to it that my Prince will want for nothing."

"T-thank you," I stammer, unable to express my deepest gratitude to her.

With a flourish of her hand, as she pockets her crystal-com, she adds darkly, "But your new legs are contingent on *if* you choose to make me your Princess. I have no doubts I am first in line as a top choice, as I am the first garland to capture your attention."

My brows furrow at this ultimatum she's giving me. "Well, Rhyanna," I start, a hint of indignation in my tone, "should I choose to make you my Princess, I think we'd be a good match—"

Rhyanna smirks. "Very well, Prince Nigel. There is no need to waste your time then, is there?—"

"However," I say, returning a cheeky smirk of my own, "you have some stiff competition?"

Rhyanna guffaws, half amused, half upset. "Oh, really? And where is this competition of mine?" she asks, peering over her shoulder. "Whom amongst my fellow garlands are you interested in?"

I clear my throat. "She is not a garland."

"I don't follow."

"But she is a Zepyterian."

Rhyanna glares at me, jaw clenched. "You cannot ask for a non-garlands hand in marriage."

"Says who?"

"Me!" Rhyanna exclaims. "Who is this Zepyterian, by the way? Is it one of the help? Has a low-wage Fairy stirred a feeling of love and splendor within your heart? Who is it so I may have them escorted out of Quill?"

"She's a Fairy who marches to the beat of her own drum," I say, heart pattering in my chest, beating faster and faster.

"Spit it out already?" This Fairy has no time for games, and she clearly lacks respect for royals.

"Windy. Her name is Windy."

Rhyanna's face blanches, pallor as white as snow. She looks as if she's about to faint from the news. "If you'll excuse me, Prince Nigel." Rhyanna waves the garlands forward, and they march down the hall, stealing looks at me, some smiling, others visibly upset by the news of Windy's first-place standing. "Let's be off, garlands. Prince Nigel has some deep thinking to do because only a Fairy with half a brain would dare stoop so low as to choose a Junkyard Fairy over me—over any of us."

I shake my head, remembering my sole mission: Find Tyeese.

I'm running again, down the hall and to Tyeese's chambers.

Chapter 18: Nigel

"Tyeese?" I call, knuckles rasping against her chamber door, strangely ajar. A void of black peeking out at me from the crack in the door. Tyeese's chamber should be guarded by Knights, ordered by my father to shield her as she is now a public figure. However, it appears as if Father has requested *all* the Knights of Quill to serve elsewhere in the Kingdom.

Since Tyeese swore an oath to Father to aid him during these unfortunate times, Tyeese is never without proper security when she ventures out of the Kingdom on her personal days. Even when Tyeese is off the Kingdom grounds, she is readily available to make a swift return. I find it unsettling that today of all days, not only is Tyeese not answering my calls, but her chamber isn't aglow with light. For Tyeese to find rest during this occasion where I am to choose a bride and where Father must appear his best is grounds for termination.

"Tyeese," I say, lifting my voice to a tone I would use for a misbehaving child. "I've given you a ring, and you've ignored my calls. I must ask that you escort me to where Father and Matriarch Xenobia are having their chat." I wait a few heartbeats, tilting my ear close to the gilded door, waiting for an answer.

My impatience gets the best of me. I burst into her darkened chambers, scanning her living quarters. I snap my fingers to summon the lights to shine, but I remain in the dark after four more snaps. The only light source in this room is the moonlight spilling cool white light on the carpet. I'm ready to give up my search as I spy Tyeese's empty bed when I see a handprint impressed on the windowpane.

"Is that..." I carefully approach the window, inspecting the print like a sleuth. I bring my face closer to the mark as my feet squelch in a puddle beneath me. I look down, lift my foot, and in that next instant, I yelp as I tumble into the spillage.

I brace myself against the bed, one hand gripping the duvet, the other pressed into the damp carpet. On my knees, I bring my hands into the moonlight, exposing a black, sticky mass on them. A shudder slips through me, screaming its way out of my mouth. My hands are covered in blood.

"T-Tyeese?" My voice is desperate, a plea to the stars that this blood doesn't belong to her.

A jewel glints near the leg of the bedpost. It's one of Tyeese's pear-shaped diamond earrings that I had gifted to her when I overheard her talking about her mother's collection of jewels. Her mother's jewelry box had been stolen the day the sun departed the Realm of Quill.

Shakily, I extend my stained hands to Tyeese's treasure, leaning forward, so my chest is level with the floor. I'm a hair away when I suddenly feel someone watching me. My eyes find those of Tyeese's. Her eyes glazed over, lifeless. Her body is stuffed under her bed as if the culprit were in a rush. Tyeese's body has been twisted in impossible angles, her arms bent awkwardly, her legs twisted and mangled.

"Tyeese..." I whisper, tears stinging my eyes. "W-what's happened to you? Who did this?"

"Hello?" a voice says from the door as it creaks open. "Is anyone in here? I heard screaming?" It's one of the servants whose name I don't know. "Hello?" they say again, snapping their fingers.

To my horror... the lights blaze alive, blinding me as the chamber is drowned in waves of golden light. I stiffen and hold my breath as if doing so will make me invisible to the naked eye. The servant's footsteps patter closer to me, their shadow climbing the walls as they near.

The fine hairs on my arms shoot upright as I shout my demands. "Don't come any closer! Please."

"P-Prince Nigel?" the curious servant says, shuffling their feet closer and closer until…

I lunge upward, my feet sliding on the slick carpet as I steady my legs. The servant, who looks about as aged as Father, whose name is on the tip of my tongue, opens her mouth to scream—to alert the entire Kingdom about the blood-covered Prince standing with their hands raised. "It's not what it seems."

The servant sucks in a breath through her mouth, reading to screech. I am bounding over the bed in an instant, bloodstained hands grasping for her. I collided with the servant's body, imprinting that of Tyeese's blood on their pristine, star-spangled white uniform. The servant's scream is muffled by my hands pressed against her mouth so hard I can feel her teeth biting into my palms.

"Remain calm," I say, affecting a twang of peace in my voice, though it's forced. The servant continues to struggle; tears flood her eyes and spill down their cheeks.

"Whatever you think I've done, please know I am innocent," I demand, pinning down the servant like a criminal. "I'm going to release my hands." I do so, removing them slowly. "But if you scream, I will have your entire family charged under the Fifth Star."

The servant quickly obliges, bobbing their head, eyes so wide, her irises are almost swallowed by the white. I couldn't think of anything else to say to her, to bring calm to this most unfortunate situation. Charging her under the Fifth Star means her entire bloodline will be wiped out. I have no intention of harming anyone. I need time to sort this mess out.

I offer to help the servant to stand. Gore-slicked fingers extended to her. The servant shakes her head, cringes away from me, and curls into one corner of the room. Hugging her legs to her chest, she sobs uncontrollably.

The servant's cry tugs at a thread of a memory I've locked away. This servant, whoever she is, has shed tears before me before. When is the question?

The servant speaks through her wailing, "P-please don't

take my family away from me. T-they are all I h-have left. I promise not to speak a word of this—of your crime."

My tone is pointed as I jab a finger in her direction. "I've nothing to do with this crime you accuse me of. To be clear, I had come to Tyeese's room to check in on her," I explain, pulling back my finger to clasp my hands together. "Tyeese failed to answer my calls—"

"So, you killed her?"

Sheer fury scrunches my nose, brows, and mouth. "Are you even listening to me? I did not kill Tyeese, for star's sake. Do you think I, your Prince and soon-to-be King, am capable of taking the life of another?"

The servant's face grimaces, her expression telling me she believes me a monster. When I glare at her, she spits in my face, an offense punishable by death. My fingers glide to my dagger. "Tara," she says, shrinking away from me as I scowl at her. "My Tara..."

Tara? I remember that name—

My bubble-com chirps. I bite my lip, not wanting to answer the call. I must focus on the servant, who I sense will make a break for it the instant I look elsewhere. The air in the room is heavy with the smell of blood, a rusted scent clogging my lungs. The servant keeps a watchful eye on me as my bubble-com buzzes and buzzes.

"Damn it," I curse. "What is it?" I implore as I unpocket my com to an image of Mikah looking frantic. The servant takes that time of distraction to hightail it out of Tyeese's room. "Speak quick, Mikah!"

I'm racing after the servant. The older woman is quick on her feet, but so are all the servants of the Kingdom. It's a requirement upon which employment in the Kingdom is extensively considered.

"There's a situation here," Mikah speaks brusquely, annoyed by something.

"Can't it wait until..." I clench my jaw hard. The servant takes off, wingbeats flapping in an erratic pattern. My wings flourish from my backside, and with a running start, I leap and fly. My artic blue wings are a blur with movement, propelling me fast ahead. But not fast enough! This servant has undoubtedly conquered the maze-like nature of the Kingdom, and therein, she has the upper hand. Had I been more interested in the hundreds of rooms throughout my home or the secret corridors the servants use to their advantage, I'd be able to figure a way to cut this chase short.

"Nigel!" Mikah squawks.

I keep my attention ahead as I round a corner, hot on the servant's tail. "What is it, Mikah?"

"You're blue-haired friend is causing a ruckus here," he says, muttering an obscenity under his breath.

"Are you talking about—" I careen into the wall near me, bounce off the window, and into a portrait of my ancestors, with their noses aloft in a snobbish manner. The portrait frame hits the floor with a crack. Stumbling to right myself, I land on my knees and elbows. "Windy." Her name is soft against my lips. "She came back," I say to myself, briefly forgetting the high-speed chase I had been on.

"Yeah, she's back all right." Mikah wipes a hand down his face. "And she has the entire Kingdom up in arms. Get here quick."

"What do you mean?"

"Your little friend is warning everyone about the… the Ogres she'd run into. This isn't good, not at all."

"Ogres?" My stars. I pray that this hectic day where I'd just found Father's caretaker dead doesn't turn into an even more horrifying event.

"Nigel," Mikah says, cheeks sagging, lips crumpling into worry. "I'm… concerned. I had thought King Nigel was off his rocker last night, but I knew deep down he was speaking the truth."

"Don't worry, Mikah," I pronounce, bolstering an air of confidence in my voice. "Everything will be all right."

Suddenly, all the lights in the hall wink out. Mikah curses

as the screams of all the attendees in the foyer pour through my com.

Footsteps thud from somewhere in the hall. "It's a blackout," I assure whomever it is slowly walking to me. "No need to worry."

Mikah's voice sounds, instructing the guests to: "Remain calm."

"Mikah, assure them I am on my way."

Mikah nods, his serious face illuminated by the soft blue light of his bubble-com, and the call ends.

My fingers hover over the holo-buttons of my com, preparing to call Tyeese when I remember she is no longer of this plane. Had Father learned how to work a bubble-com, I'd have no problem reaching him and sharing the awful news of Tyeese's death. Not only are there Ogres in Quill, but there is a murderer in the Kingdom.

Twinkling starlight trickles through the floor-to-ceiling windows, slicing through most of the dark in the corridor. A figure looms thirty to thirty-five feet from me, its face obscured by the darkness as it slowly approaches.

"Is it you?" I ask, thinking of the servant that got away. "If you hadn't noticed, something strange is happening, and that should ease your mind... well, in the case I am a murdering Prince."

The figure chuckles, a masculine intonation to it. This isn't the female servant I had been trailing. Slinking into a stream of starlight, a face like my own—like Father's with those hereditary green eyes—smiles at me. It's as if I am looking at an older version of myself, taller, leaner, and crueler.

Rubbing my eyes, I shake my head. "This isn't real. This isn't real."

"Oh, but it is." The figure chortles.

The corridor lights bloom alive, shredding the dark to nothingness and revealing the strange-looking Ogre before me. My hands are quick as I reach for my trusty dagger, fingers sticky with blood. I swipe at the foul imitator, hungry to spill his blood and save my Kingdom. The Ogre dodges left and right, then grabs hold of my wrist and squeezes until I release my dagger from my grasp, clattering on the carpet.

"How rude of you, Nephew," the Ogre says, canines glinting. "Is this how you treat one of your own?"

"Let go of me, you abomination!" I swing my free hand at the Ogre, knuckles hungry for a fist-to-cheek connection.

The Ogre tilts his head back and grins as my punch misses. "Nephew," he says cheekily. The Ogre with Father's face pulls me in close by my hand and whispers, "Why so serious? All I am here for is to open your Fairy eyes to the truth about *everything!*"

"Get off of me, you beast!" It's a struggle to free myself from his hold. "I have no time for your lies. You deserve death; all you Ogres deserve death—

All my animosity and hatred swirl in confusion as the Ogre unveils his wings—his Fairy wings to me. Ogres don't have wings, do they?

His massive wings nearly fill the corridor, swirling with blues and whites—familial colors that only the males born to the Cloud line possess. I work my agape mouth to say... something. What that something is? I don't quite know.

"Who are you?" I ask, scrutinizing his features: half-ogre, half-fairy. He is a semi-perfect mixture of my kind and those green beasts, even sharing their green flesh.

Rolling his eyes at me and releasing my hand, the Ogre introduces himself: "Neven Cloud."

It's as if the breath has been punched from my lungs. I'm swept into a whirlwind of questions that need answers. Father had revealed to me last night I had an Uncle I never knew about, who sided with Ogre-kind for reasons unexplained. But that doesn't negate the fact that my Uncle looks like an Ogre in the flesh. How is that possible? Perhaps it's a curse? Maybe he subjected himself to some sort of skin grafting experiment?

"I can sense that your mind is reeling from this revelation," Neven says, tilting his head to one side. Neven—my

Uncle—flares his nostrils. "My horde is here. Let's be on our way, shall we?"

"What is it that you want from us? Is it the throne? Gold? Revenge?"

"I want only two things," Neven states, holding up two vomit-green fingers. "The throne, well, yes. It is mine by birthright alone. However, the most important of the two is the daughter I share with Jordana. The stars are ever in my favor on this joyous occasion: Jordana is in attendance in the Kingdom. Invading Zepyteria had been our next task, but *this* has worked itself out all too splendidly."

"Jordana?" I blink, confused, then gasp. "Matriarch Xenobia?"

Chapter 19: Windy

I was accosted by the Knights of Quill. Their shimmering armor, embossed with five-pointed stars that trail from their helmets to their breastplates, gave me sickening flashbacks to a time I want to heal from. The news I had to share shan't be hindered by these Knights. I had to warn them.

The entire party swelled into a frenzy after I'd dropped a bomb on them.

"Ogres!" I shouted until my voice was hoarse, my chest heaved, and my legs throbbed from overexertion. I'd run all the way here only to be tossed into a corner by a guard, their sword unsheathed, brows pinched.

"Lies," the guard shouted, "there are no Ogres—"

Then the lights were snuffed out that next instant. A cacophony of terrified screams erupted all around me, and a stampede of Garlands and Quillians rushed every which way. I used that time, the distraction, to slip away, jostling other Fairies on my way to find an exit in the pitch black.

"Remain calm!" a voice hollered above the noise, but no one listened.

I was shoved and pushed, throttled around like a boat battered by a thunderstorm at sea, until the lights burst back to life. The foyer was illuminated again, the dazzling white light seeming to trigger a tranquilizing effect. Every Fairy halted in their tracks. The looks on their faces were all screwed with an amalgam of equal parts fear and confusion.

Then the fear won out and exploded through every Fairy—through me, too—as we realized we were all surrounded by cloaked figures. About fifty of them. They blocked all the exits; some stood on the upper levels, peering down from the balustrade, their arms folded, hoods obscuring the faces I knew to be Ogre. Although we Fairies outnumbered them greatly, we dared not move a muscle.

The King of Quill appeared from behind a door, arm in arm with Matriarch Xenobia. Although the two royals seemed bewildered by the commotion, aghast expressions smeared on their faces, I had this sneaking suspicion they knew more than meets the eye. The lack of urgency in their steps struck me as strange as they entered the foyer. It was as if the Ogres were vermin to be shooed away.

The King was about to speak to his uninvited guest, causing dissension, when Prince Nigel appeared with the Ogre I'd met not too long ago. He walked with his head bowed, his black hair falling across his face. His hands and clothing were caked in blood. I lurched forward, waiting to aid him in any way I could, to tend to his wounds, but I stopped myself. That blood wasn't his. And it didn't belong to the familiar-looking Ogre trailing in the Prince's wake.

It then hit me like a sack of dirty socks to the skull, connecting the twisted, confused thoughts in my mind: The King, Prince Nigel, and that Ogre all share the same features. The green of their eyes, the tar-kissed hair, the cheekbones, even the way they walked. This Ogre was related to them. Judging by the Prince's exhausted demeanor, I could tell he had discovered something Realm shattering.

***

King Nigel raises his hand high, rousing the cacophonic gathering of petrified Garlands and furious Quillians. The Garlands accused the Quillians of leading them to their doom, blindsiding them with a coming Ogre attack. The Quillians deflected such claims, assuring us unwanted visitors from Zepyteria the Ogres were the doing of their enemies. And that enemy being the Fairies hailing from the Realm of the eternal sun.

I found it odd that every Fairy thought this a proper time

to argue and toss accusations around when there are puffing Ogres lingering about. If anything, we should question the King about all of this. Does no one but me see the family resemblance between the Ogre and the royal family?

As I peer at the Ogre with the King's face, delighted by the calamity that his kind has inflicted on the entire party, it's all too obvious now. That Ogre is half Fairy, half Ogre. It's undeniable.

I swing my curious eyes about, studying the other hooded Ogres, exploring their features, when the King of Quill shouts.

"SILENCE!"

The foyer is blanketed in unsteady silence.

"Fellow Quillians and our Zepyterian guests," the King says, a contrived smile on his expressionless face. "I ask for order this instant." The King whistles a sharp note, and the Knights, with their swords unsheathed, dispersed through the foyer to block all possible exits.

Why has the King ordered his knights to stand guard near the doors? I have this sickening feeling that something horrible is about to happen—not just to the Ogres, but to us Fairies. I slip away from the crowd, searching for a dark corner where I can phone for Mister Ed to tell him I may never see him again.

"What is the meaning of this, Father?" Prince Nigel asks through gritted teeth. "Why are you so calm when there are Ogres in our home? When one amongst them has slaughtered Tyeese!"

The Ogre, who I'm surmising is the leader of his Ogre brood, chuckles. "Do you truly believe one of my kind..." the Ogre shakes his head, then reiterates, "Excuse me—one of *our* kind would commit such a monstrous act? Perhaps you should ask your Father what happened to Tyeese. My brother has an affinity for spilling blood."

"Brother?" every Fairy echoes, the word reverberating through each of us, drowning the room in a swirling, baffling vortex.

The King whistles again, and much to their confusion, the knights raise their swords threateningly. All but a few knights refuse the King's demand. The King shakes his head, then snaps his fingers at a male Fairy in the crowd.

"Mikah," the King says, "congratulations on your promotion to Commander." Mikah's jaw drops in utter disbelief. "Now, please escort those members of the Quillian Knights who dare to oppose me to the prisons."

Mikah nods his blond head. "Yes, my King."

"No! Don't!" Prince Nigel ambles to Mikah, a desperate look in his eyes. "Mikah, you mustn't—"

"Do as I say, Mikah, or you will face the same fate." The King grins, and that nasty grin is enough to tell me that Quill is ruled by a crazy maniac.

Mikah looks from the Prince to the King. "I... I thank you, my King. It has been a dream of mine to lead the Quillian knights." With a flourish of his robes, Mikah spins to face the Knights who've disregarded the King's orders. "You three," he says, pointing with a wavy dagger in each of the Knight's direction. "You are under arrest for insubordination of the highest order. As with such a crime, you will all be sentenced to death."

Mikah jerks his head to one side. The Knights creep forward to the King, heads low. Removing their swords and helmets and planting their equipment at the king's feet, the dishonored Knights are escorted to the prisons by their new Commander in charge: Mikah.

"Are you finished with the evasive tactics, brother?" the Ogre asks, feigning a yawn. "I think your court would love to know all about me. Go on, tell them who I truly am."

The King speaks, but not to his Ogre-brother, to every Fairy in the foyer. "I ask that every Fairy of the court relinquish any communication devices and weapons of any kind. From this moment forward, you are all prisoners of Quill."

A rush of motion breaks out, and some Fairy lunges for the King, screaming words I dare not repeat. Others follow, begging the King to release them from this hell. Even the Garlands are yelling at the King; some hurl questions to the Matriarch, who has been as still as stone ever since that Ogre pranced in.

"Girls," the Matriarch says above the din, voice unsteady, "please remain calm. Everything will be all right, I promise."

A Fairy's guttural scream cuts through the noise as their body falls to the ground, a puddle of blood pooling around them as a Knight removes his sword from their back. Another Knight takes the Fairy's bubble-com, cracks it against the floor, and steps on it with their iron-clad feet, shattering it to pieces.

"Should any of you refuse," the King says, inspecting the crowd, "you will be met with death. Is that understood? Now, I beg you all to be silent as I try to explain the reason for our Ogre visitors. Before we begin, though, I must ask again that you forfeit your communication devices. No news of this shall leave the Kingdom. Is that understood? If any of this gets out, all the Realms of Nasturtium will be overwrought with hysteria. I'd wish to avoid that by any means necessary."

There's a stiffness shared between all the Fairies before they eventually surrender their communication devices. The Knights coil through the room, appropriating bubble-coms and crystal-coms. The King observes his cavalry, and with a swish of his finger, he gestures to a rose-gold hearth crackling with flames. Acknowledging their King, the knights toss each communication device they've collected on their walkthrough into the burning ruby fire before circling back around the foyer. I watch in shared horror at the faces of the young Fairies whose entire lives revolve around their coms twist into pain and sadness.

Quickly, I press myself against the far wall, beside a table of sweet-smelling, untouched deserts. Luckily for me, Mister Ed is my only contact. That eliminates the need for endless scrolling, like other Fairies who have an abundance of friends. I tap Mister Ed's name on the screen, clutching the crystal in the palm of my hand.

I flick my eyes up for a second, checking the Knights. They're getting closer. I need to tell Mister Ed what's going on, to tell him I love him so much. That I'm sorry for being a brat.

And... and... I'll promise to be a better daughter. As my thoughts race and a Knight spots me on my com, our eyes meeting for the briefest of moments, I think perhaps Mister Ed was right. I had spent all my life in the Junkyard, experiencing an all too comfortable life when I could've been out and about living it up. Instead, I chose the Junkyard over everything. It was my safe haven, the only place in the Realms where I could just... be.

Mister Ed's com rings and rings and rings. The Knights shove through the crowd, tossing aside garlands on his way to me.

To kill me.

The ringing stops, and a face appears on my com. I know this face. It's a face that will never leave the blackness of my closed eyes. I had thought I had dreamed that day I was with Amana when the Dragons appeared at the window.

"Windy," the Dragon-man says, "I'm afraid your Father is busy at the moment." He chuckles darkly as the connection cuts out.

There's a scream from somewhere around me. I look up in time to see the Knight and his gleaming sword arching through the air to cut me down.

"NO!" a voice shouts as I roll out of the way, the sword catching the ends of my blue locs. My wings burst open—flapping hard but doing little to lift me off my feet.

"Leave her alone!" Was that Prince Nigel? "This is a direct order from your Prince!"

A shadow looms overhead as the Prince tackles the Knight. The Knight's sword flails into the air. The blade comes spiraling down, metal gleaming, before it pins me to the wall by my left wing.

The sound that ripples from me is a noise all too familiar. It's a sound that was ripped from my core each time I had been abused by the Keepers. Punished by their swords, beaten by their fists, stomped by their sabatons.

Kicking and screaming, my left wing gives way to my weight and thrashing as it splits in half. Everything goes blurry, and I brace for the impact as I fall to the floor. A set of arms catches me and wraps themselves around my back and legs. My wings judder as they slip back to their safe place.

"Are you all right, Windy?" Prince Nigel holds me close to his chest. I can hear his heartbeat—it thumps against my head. Smell the tang of blood on his clothing. A strange sensation takes hold of me. I can only describe it as one of comfort. Something about how he holds me so dearly makes the pain strumming through my wings melt away. He exhales a long breath when I nod. The Prince balances me in his hands, his legs creaking as he turns to face his court and the Ogres on standby.

"Neven," Prince Nigel says, tone stone-cold, "tell me what you are doing in my Kingdom. Tell me why you've stolen the cleansing crystal, depriving us Quillians of freshwater. Tell me everything my Father refuses to."

Through my blurry vision, I watch as the King shifts uncomfortably as the Ogre matching his height beside him prepares to speak.

King Nigel bellows like a crazed bovid. "You and all your Ogres will die here—" the King lunges for the Ogre, his frail physique moving with such speed, I'm surprised this old Fairy was capable of such fluid mobility.

The King misses his mark and falls into the arms of a Knight, saving him from face-planting. In a flash of cerulean and powder white, the Ogre's wings bloom from him. How can such a nasty creature like an Ogre own such marvelous wings?

Every Fairy's jaw drops, and unhinged gasps leave their agape mouths. Whispers that hurriedly erupt into shouts fuel the party with a hunger for the truth!

Who is this Ogre? Why is he here? And What does he want?

Chapter 20: Nigel

"How splendid it is to have what would've been my court revel in my presence." My Ogre Uncle Neven proclaims, waving his hand in a sweeping motion. Aloft above the court, the Ogre smirks at the hysteria he's evoking.

Father is tended to by his Knights as they escort him to his throne. His face is marred with a fury I've never beholden in all my years. Even when he was upset with the distressing decisions I've made in my life and the harmless lies I told to cover my rear, he's always kept calm. Be that as it may, I now view my Father through a different lens. He ordered a Knight to slay a Quillian in cold blood. Demanded my friend—and new Commander—Mikah to have innocent lives snuffed out for refusing to oblige their King. Sure, it *is* an insubordinate act, but Father has become a ruthless ruler. Incomprehensibly so.

Perhaps... perhaps he was always this way. Perhaps my Ogre Uncle hovering above the throng is the answer to all the burning questions I've always wanted to ask Father.

In my arms, Windy's head lolls to one side, her face wincing from the pain of her injured wing. Windy fits perfectly in my arms, her body nestled against my chest, our breaths in sync. I feel a set of eyes on me, searing a hole in the back of my head. Turning slightly, I interlace gazes with Rhyanna, who snaps her attention upward and away from me.

"I am Neven Cloud," Neven continues, his wings beating slowly. "Son of Miriam and Nigel Cloud I, former Queen, and King of Quill. I was their firstborn, their ugly duckling of a son. For my first four years of life, I was hidden from the public eye and subjected to... experiments to find a cure. Mother thought her womb to be cursed. Thought the sins of all her Fairy ancestors had finally caught up to her. But it was my Father, Nigel, who knew the truth. I was tossed out of the Kingdom, a babe who had to learn quickly how to survive. Luckily, I was adopted by a band of Ogres who—"

"Enough!" Father comes to his feet, body trembling from rage or his sickness. "You are a liar—a deceiver—here to wrought chaos and ruin. I shall have you slain like the beast you are—"

"Like the beasts *WE* are, brother!" In a flash of movement, my Uncle swoops down to Father and rips Father's robes to shreds in a blur of motion.

As if we Fairies haven't gasped enough today or haven't experienced a wild array of emotions, we are all moved into shock.

"Feast your eyes on this!" Neven is airborne again, avoiding the swipe of swords hunting him down.

Father gathers his shredded robes, desperately trying to hide the green chest, heaving heavy breaths. "It's not what you think," Father says, voice cracking. "It's a curse... it's..."

I find it surprising that words of any kind elude even the most verbose being I know. It's unlike him to see defeat. I had thought the only time Father would ever be down and out was when the reaper would come to take his soul.

A gaggle of whispers moves around me. Curious garlands want to know if I am like Father. If I am blighted with the tinge of monstrous green like an Ogre.

"I am not an Ogre," I protest amongst the growing questions and the concerned glances.

"Oh, but you are, Nephew." I squeeze Windy tighter in my arms as Neven descends. Neven taps at my wooden leg with the tip of his boot.

"I was born without legs," I say, avoiding the cringing sensation tightening my shoulders and abdomen. I've never spoken those words aloud, not to myself nor to other Fairies. Shame has always had a grapple on me from the day I knew I was... different.

"That is a fallacy." My brutish Uncle leans forward, his lips dangerously close to my ears. "Ask your Father what happened to your legs." When Neven stands to his full height, I shake my head.

"Father is not the type to share secrets."

"Nor was my Father—your Grandfather." Neven claps his hands, and his Ogre horde removes their hoods, exposing their Ogre faces. Full-blooded Ogre faces with prominent brows, thick and full, some with bulbous noses, others adorned with a single horn at the center of their heads. "I'd hate to get between a Father and son, so I'll leave it up to you, Nephew, if you want to engage your tight-lipped Father about the truth. I came here for one thing; however, now that I've seen my former love, Jordana, in attendance, I guess it is time to put it all on the table."

Neven prances through the crowd, his massive wings jostling the court. "Brother, what I want from you is what is rightfully mine by birthright: the throne of Quill. From there, my brood and I will reclaim the realm of Quill as Ogre territory. Not that it was ever Fairy territory—" Neven whirls around dramatically and points to a young Fairy shivering in the crowd. "You! What have your teachers, parents, and news media taught you about the Fairy Realms?"

The young Fairy slips away behind the leg of their parent.

Someone from the crowd answers Neven's question. "That the Fairy Realms were bestowed to all Fairy-kind by the grace of the Gods and Goddesses who once ruled." It's Rhyanna. She boldly saunters to Neven, her head held high, black hair swaying at her back. "They saw us lesser Fairies worthy of claiming Nasturtium as our own."

"And what of Ogres, hmm?" Neven asks, brows kissing his hairline. "What have you learned about Ogres?"

Rhyanna answers: "We were *all* taught Ogres were akin to demons. Your kind had been jealous of the favor the Gods showered us Fairies and traveled from the pit of Parnissi to devour the hearts of the innocents." Rhyanna tosses her hair over her shoulder. "Ogres are what Lions are to lambs, what fire is to a garden, what disease is to a body."

Neven cackles, smiling wide. "How wrong you are. How wrong you all are." In a flash of blue and white, Neven takes to the air once more. His wings flap furiously as he speaks. "Nasturtium, long ago, belonged to Ogres and Ogres alone. It wasn't until Fairies invaded our world, seeking refuge, that Ogres fell. My Ogre ancestors fed your hungry, bathed your dirty, and provided them a place to slumber. And then... then the true nature of Fairy-kind reared its ugly head. But enough about that. I am here to claim my throne and find my daughter born from my once beloved Jordana."

"Don't you dare drag me into your lies, Ogre!" Matriarch Xenobia points an accusatory finger at Neven, white teeth flashing. "It is time you and your horde crawl back to the mountains of Hraylor like the insects you are."

"We could've had something special, you and I." Neven shrugs, tosses his hands as if releasing all his past memories into the ether. "You promised me so many things in the heat of passion. I was a fool to believe you loved me. A fool to believe that we could resurrect Namanzi with our daughter. You hungered to fix the Realms like I did. But you resort to sacrificing your own to override Namanzi's blessing so that your Zepyterians can water their measly crops."

"You're a liar!" Matriarch Xenobia screams.

"No, he's not." Windy slips from my arms to remove a crumpled sheet of paper from her dress pocket. "Neven," she summons my Uncle to her side. Windy doesn't flinch when my Uncle descends to her side and takes the paper from her hand. While Neven's eyes dart back and forth as he reads whatever is on that slip, Windy says accusingly, "You're a murderer, Matriarch Xenobia. Amana told me. She told me everything. But at least you were honest about your affair with Madeline."

Matriarch Xenobia's pale face goes nearly translucent. "Y-You wretched thing you. I should've had you killed—"

"Madeline?" Neven repeats the name as if it's a familiar taste on his tongue. "Yes. Yes. I know her. She was the Fairy who stole my child from me. Who are you, Fairy?"

"My name is Windy! Don't you forget it. I—" There's something else Windy wanted to say, but those words are lost as she glares at the Matriarch as if she weren't a royal.

"I've had enough of this!" Father's wings ignite to life, whirling a thunderstorm of colors. A vial appears in Father's hand, sloshing with red liquid. This alerts Neven, who dives for him. Father is a moment away from imbibing the liquid when Neven smacks it from his hand. The vial disunites, breaking against the floor.

Neven grips Father by the throat and yanks him close. "For a Fairy who *chooses* to have wither infect his body—a curable disease Ogres can only be afflicted with—you move rather quickly, brother."

I'm unable to dissect that bit of information as knights descend upon Neven, swords ready to strike to save their King. Father quickly raises a hand as Neven murmurs something only he can hear.

"I-I surrender." Father crumples to his hands and knees. He looks to his court and bobs his head. "Do it. Surrender or all will be lost."

Every Fairy obliges, prostrating themselves before Neven, all but a few who are as lost as I am. Windy backs into me, her wide brown eyes seeking an answer from me I do not have.

Matriarch Xenobia remains upright, her dress flowing around her as if caught in a maelstrom. "We can overpower him, King Nigel. He's but an Ogre with a few cockroaches at his command."

"N-No." Father shakes his head. "He... He will kill *them* all."

"What are you talking about..." Matriarch Xenobia takes a step back, mouth tightening, hands curling into fists. "Don't you touch them. Don't you even try to—"

"Or what?" Neven beams, arms folded along his chest. "I will kill all the Humans if I have to."

"Humans?" I breathe against my fingers glued to my lips.

"Humans are but a myth."

Neven flashes me a look of pity. "Nephew, you have so much to learn." He fixes his attention on Matriarch Xenobia. "Tell me where my daughter is."

"Never!" Matriarch Xenobia's mien, compacted as if being smushed together, flares scarlet and crimson with a rage that startles me.

"Very well." My Uncle looks to one of his Ogres, who happily steps forward and bows to him. The Ogre is a slender male whose dark robes are much too large for him. Their skin is a grassy green, hair is a vibrant neon yellow. "Show me the threads, Bur'Vis."

Bur'Vis's deep brown eyes are consumed by an abysmal blackness as breathlessly mesmerizing as it is frightening. The Ogre sweeps his large finger in a circle from the Matriarch, who swats the Ogre's pointer finger away and points at Windy standing beside me.

"Her," Bur'Vis announces, holding his head, mouth scrunched in pain. "She has the key to unlock the hiding place of your dear daughter, which is protected by magic cast by Jordana. That magic can be temporarily disturbed by that blue-haired Fairy. She knows the location of the key!"

Windy checks her surroundings before pointing at herself. "*Me?* I don't know where your daughter is. And I don't have any keys to give you."

"Are you sure about this, Bur'Vis?" Neven stares curiously at Windy, skeptical. "Windy. I have a job for you—"

"Puff no," Windy says, "I'm not working for you."

Bur'Vis clears his throat. "Perhaps you'll do it for your guardian, then?" Bur'Vis's black eyes peer into Windy. "How bizarre," Bur'Vis says, "he's being held prisoner by Dragonborn males. Nasturtium was once ruled by the Dragonborn eons ago, but that's history for a later time. Two Dragon males appear to be waiting for Windy's return." He speaks that last sentence to Neven.

"Dragonborn, you say?" Neven's eyes bulge in surprise.

"How bizarre, indeed. So, Windy, how's about it? It seems as if you're needed at home, anyway."

Windy acquiesces and wipes hot tears from her eyes. "What is it you want? A key? Is that it? Okay. I'll find this key for you. But I need to check on my Dad first. Then I'll bring you the key. I promise."

"Then it's settled," Neven says, extending his hand to Windy. "I shall grant you three days to return to me with the key. Which is a generous amount of time. I don't have the patience to wait forever. For I have plans for all of Nasturtium. And those plans will exclude you and others of your choosing should you complete the task I've asked of you. I will reward you with something extra special that will be yours and yours alone."

"Deal," Windy says.

"Wait!" I dash as fast as my wooden legs can carry me to face Neven. "I will not stand idle while Windy risks her life to retrieve some key for you."

"I'm not risking my life," Windy scoffs, rolling her eyes. "I'm simply going to bring your Uncle-Ogre a key. Wherever that key is, I'll figure it out."

"Neven." I square my shoulders and straighten my spine. "As it is written: Quillian law allows for a duel to the death for the throne between members of the royal Cloud family. A duel hasn't occurred in over three hundred years since twins Nassem and Nassir were born. Nassem had challenged Nassir to engage in a deadly duel. And although Nassir was first born by a few minutes and by birth alone was the rightful heir, he accepted the challenge because he knew his brother was ill-prepared to rule Quill. It was Nassir's arrogance that cost him his life. Thus, Nassem was crowned King. Since you've usurped the throne from my Father in a matter of seconds, I promise you I shall reclaim what is rightfully mine. Be prepared for the fight of your life."

"If that's what you desire, Prince," Neven hisses between his teeth. "I shall spill your blood happily to defend *my* throne. But, to prove your worth, I'd love for you to bring me the scale of a Dragonborn. Had I known we had Dragonborns visiting Nasturtium, I'd be able to tap into powers unknown. However, I think you need the Dragon scale more than I do because the only way you, Nigel, will ever be able to defeat me is by consuming one.

"I accept your challenge, Nephew. Now, be off you two. It's time to celebrate my coronation. Rise all of you. Let's have a party, shall we? We will celebrate for three days and two nights. No one is permitted to leave my Kingdom but Windy and Prince Nigel."

Music swells around the foyer, calamitous and unfitting for such an unsettling chain of events. Still bowed at Neven's feet, Father is uncrowned as Neven slips Father's bejeweled corona atop his head. A transfer of power so quick every Fairy must accept this change. But it's only temporary.

I shall return to Quill once I slay a Dragonborn. Creatures I thought to be of mythos—who are somehow connected to the blue-haired Fairy I will join on this outlandish adventure.

Windy takes my hand in hers and squeezes it tight. A flush of heat trails up my arm. "Come on," she says, voice quavering, "we've got work to do!"

Chapter 21: Windy

What the Puff did I get myself into? Better yet, what in the entire Puff just happened? First, the lights go out, then the Ogres appear. Then the leader of the Ogres, Neven, claims he's a descendant of the Cloud lineage. Well, I don't think "claims" is the right word to use since Neven *is* the spitting image of the King and Prince. There's no denying the three males are kin.

Yet there's one thing I cannot bend my mind to understand: if Neven is half-ogre, half-fairy, then does that mean the same is true for Prince Nigel? Much to my horror, the King was disrobed—his flat, green chest with tufts of hair in places I wish I could scrub from my brain, prove he's half-Ogre. However, Nigel appears to be full Fairy from what I'm observing.

I don't mean to peek, but the Prince and I are temporarily on standby as the Prince is aided by his servants, as they strip him of his blood-caked clothing and wipe a damp towel on his face and hands. We're outside Prince Nigel's former home near a starlit pathway, crowded with mule-drawn carriages and Zepyterian unicorns. The smells of animal manure waft around us. Puff, this smell is making me queasy!

I turn my back to Nigel and his servants as his pants come down. His firm, pale cheeks wiggle from his pants, tight and firm and—

I slap my hand over my eyes. "Whoa!" I choke out. "A little warning would've been nice." Gulping thickly, I slightly part my fingers and blush. The Prince is free of the Ogre green. I had to make sure, naturally. Because... well...

Mikah shoves past me as if I were invisible and not in the middle of the pathway. "Prince Nigel." He bows formally. "I will escort you on this journey with that lesser Fairy." Mikah flashes me a disgusted look, fingers tapping the hilt of a sword at his hip.

"I think we're good," I say smarmily, crumpling my dress in my hands.

Nigel nods at me. "Windy is right." He slips on a black shirt that hugs his abs. "And she's not a lesser Fairy. She's..." Nigel wets his lips and softly exhales. "Windy is special. And besides, Mikah, I need you here. I have a job for you." Nigel claps his hands like the royal he is, and his servants vanish back inside the Ogre-infested Kingdom.

"You are the only Fairy I trust who can get the job done." Nigel palms his hands on Mikah's shoulders. I swear for an instant, a swirl of crimson stained Mikah's cheeks. But I shake my head. "While we're under siege, and I am away on my mission to aid Windy and slay a Dragonborn, I require your sleuthing abilities. Someone murdered Tyeese in her chambers —"

Mikah grits his teeth. "Isn't it obvious, Nigel? An Ogre slew Tyeese."

"In my heart—" Nigel sniffles. "—I don't believe that to be true."

Mikah regards his Prince conspiratorially. "What did that Neven say to you? Has he infected your mind with Ogre rambling that you refuse to believe what those beasts are capable of?"

"What would be their intentions for killing her?" Nigel asks, giving Mikah a shake.

"Ogres are monsters—"

"Then you believe me to be a monster as well?" Nigel's hands fall to his side. He angles his head to accentuate his neck, veins pulsing. I shudder.

A small part of me desires to plant soft kisses on his long neck.

Gosh. What the Puff is up with me?

Nigel continues, straightening his spine. "You and everyone in attendance know my family's secret. A secret I had no wits about. A secret Father kept behind his tight lips. I have Ogre blood coursing through my very veins as we speak. Does that make me a monster in your eyes? I ask you this as my best friend?"

Mikah, flustered by this question from Nigel, erupts into palpable anger. "I could've gone my whole life unknowing of your... your sickness. But now, *yes*, my Prince, I am conflicted beyond words. I swore fealty to the King when I was ten years of age, and now... now I am unsure of what the hell I am doing. I feel betrayed."

"As do I." Nigel closes the space between him and Mikah, but Mikah shoves the Prince away.

"I am certain of one thing." Mikah snickers. Dangerous, menacing energy shudders through the Fairy. "I bow to no Ogre. Half or full. Believe me, Nigel, there may be no Kingdom for you to return to."

In a flurry of motion, Nigel swings his fists at Mikah. Left hooks and rights, all failing to land their target as Mikah dodges so swiftly; it's as if he's one with the wind swirling around us. Then Mikah goes for the low blow: he sweeps Nigel off his feet. There's a cracking sound as Nigel lands with a *thud* on his back.

"Hey!" I shout, rushing over to foolishly jump in between the two. "Is this how you treat someone you love?" I shove Mikah, who doesn't evade my hands.

Mikah spits at my boots. "Love is for the weak." Smiling victoriously, Mikah unlatches his sword from his belt, and the sheath and blade clatter to the ground. "You'll be needing this, my Prince." Mikah gestures to his weapon. "You have no chance against a Dragonborn, so I'll offer you some help. I doubt you'll make it back alive, though. But don't you worry, Nigel. I'll ensure the Kingdom of Quill is well cared for in your absence. I will defeat Neven, dethrone your Father, effectively crowing myself as King of Quill."

"Y-You can't do t-that." Nigel fumbles to regain his footing, but his prosthetics are twisted in a way that will not hold his full weight. "It's a deplorable betrayal I will never forgive you for. Not in this life or the next!"

"Then you should kill me right now. Or stay on the ground where a halfling belongs."

I kick up the sword. It twirls in the air twice before I catch the hilt and point the sheath at Mikah. "Leave him alone."

"Or what?" Mikah squishes his nose against the edge of the sheath. He and I engage in the stare-off of all stare-offs. When I do nothing, he sniffs. "I've never put my hands on a female, but I'm so tempted to. You should count your blessings, Windy."

"If you're feeling froggy," I say, mimicking a swordsman's stance I've seen in illustrations, "then jump."

Mikah's eyes flash with something like admiration for me. "I don't have time for this." He turns his back to me. "Hey, Nigel, you best pray I am slain before you return because I will hold nothing back against you—freak!" With his departing words, Mikah's wings, shiny and violet, curved with snaking vines, break free in a magical display. A blast of wind trails Mikah as he takes off into the starry night.

***

Lady Donna, our unicorn chauffeur we requisitioned, sparkling as white as snow native to the Hraylor mountains, drifts through the radiant skies of Quill on our way to Zepyteria. Prince Nigel and I are in his resplendent personal carriage, furnished with a mini cooler filled with bubbly beverages. Beneath ultra-cozy seats, there are compartments stocked with mouthwash, body creams, candies, and fuzzy slippers. In the middle of the red oak flooring, projected a few feet off the floor, a map of Nasturtium buzzes and flickers in and out of view. A blinking red dot slowly moves along the map, and a squiggly line connects the Palace of Quill to my home—a small, unregistered blob.

Prince Nigel sits in a reclined chair, watching me tend to his legs. The apprehensive look on his face is enough to tell me he is uncomfortable. I blink my eyes at him, sigh, drop his legs, and scoot my back against the seat behind me.

"I can fix your legs, but it won't be my best work," I say, reaching my hand to dig into the ice-filled mini-cooler. I unearth a few selections of beverages I've never heard of—they must be native to Quill—and decide on a blue, fizzy drink. "With our limited time, I can't promise you'll be ready to take on a Dragonborn. Let alone take on your Uncle or that dastardly Mikah. Mikah is a piece of work, I'll tell you."

Prince Nigel twists his lips, then shakes his head. Pointing, he says, "You'll find extra legs for me in that drawer. My backups. I always have my carver prepare two extra pairs."

Opening the drawer, I roll my eyes. "You need legs that are more, you know, up-to-date." I pick up the polished wooden prosthetics and lay them flat near me. "I created a titanium tibia for my Dragonfly, Tinker. I'm sure I can craft something extra special for you, but, again, time isn't our friend."

I roll Nigel's pant legs up, prepared to swap out his legs, when he stops me. His hand atop mine, warm. Our eyes meet, and my body goes hot. Nigel has the most beautiful green eyes I've ever seen. I think to myself, for a laughable moment, *his eyes are green because he's part Ogre.*

"You have a Dragonfly? For a pet?" Prince Nigel asks as his fingers grasp his right upper thigh, unstrapping a black fastener. I chuckle and nod as I hand him his extra right leg. He centers his right prosthetic and stretches out his thigh, attempting to adjust it before strapping it to himself.

"She's technically not my pet," I say, guiding his hands and helping him with the fasteners. "Tinker is her own Dragonfly. She comes and goes as she pleases. I feed and wash her, but she's never around long unless she needs something. Puff-Puff, my Dragon, is my pet. He's the squishiest thing ever—"

"Dragon?" Prince Nigel shakes his head. "You have a pet Dragon? I thought Dragons went extinct a millennia ago. How do you hide a behemoth like that inside of your Junkyard?"

A laugh moves through me, giddy and relaxing. "Puff-Puff has this abnormality that keeps him the size of a balloon. He's my forever baby Dragon."

Left leg in hand, Prince Nigel regards me with a questioning gaze. "You're amazing." A rush of apple red fills his face as he quickly bows his head to hide his burning cheeks. But it's too late; I caught the Prince red-handed—err, red-faced—and all. Does the Prince... does he like me?

Being that I am a Fairy who can be uncomfortably straightforward in my approach, I ask, "Why're you all red in the face, Prince?"

"Because," he says, slowly lifting his head, sweeping his hair back from his eyes, "I believe you are the *one* for me."

I grit my teeth and scooch back a bit.

Hey, I wanted an honest answer, and the Prince gave me one. Now I'm acting all offended when, in reality, I am honored. This situation—being in close quarters with a male Fairy on a questionable voyage for an Ogre—is not your typical romantic setting. It's not a setting I never thought I'd find myself in.

I think my quiet has offended Prince Nigel because he shies away from me, picks up his discarded legs, and stands them up under the carriage window. "I didn't mean to cause you any distress," he says as I open my mouth to speak. "It was thoughtless of me to speak such nonsense—"

"It's not nonsense if you believe it to be true." Hiding my hands behind my back, I swing my gaze everywhere but to him. "I-I mean, I... I may feel the same way, but it's too early to tell. Besides, I wouldn't be a good catch. Did you see those other garlands? I don't look like them. I don't come from a wealthy family like they do. What you see, Prince Nigel, is what you get. Hypothetically speaking, if we were to flirt with this idea, I would have nothing to bring to the table. I didn't finish secondary school. Never had dreams of going to college, really. I'm just a Fairy from the Junkyard."

Nigel assesses his new legs, rolling his feet back and forth from heel to forefoot before he stands. He tucks his hands behind his back and stands a hairsbreadth away from me. "You say you have nothing to bring to the table, Windy. Yet, I can only imagine the table you'll be able to craft from the finds in your Junkyard. That's the kind of mate I am seeking, in truth. Had things not turned into the hellish Ogre nightmare it had, I wouldn't have had ample time to select the right Fairy for me. I would've chosen a mate based solely on first impressions. Since you weren't a garland, I'd have to choose another. I would've regretted my decision for all eternity. I am thrilled, however, to have this chance to get to know you. Truthfully, I am scared about what the future holds. And if there is a future for my Kingdom. With everything up in the air and tomorrow never promised, why not? Why not you and me? Why not now?"

"I literally just met you today," I feign a scoff, leveling my eyes with his dangerous viper green eyes. "How can you hold so many emotions for me after only a day?" How can I say this to him when I agree with everything he's said? When I feel what he's feeling. Maybe it's the thrill—the uncertainty, too—of the adventure soon to come that has us confiding our deepest thoughts with one another.

Tomorrow isn't promised.

Prince Nigel's chest deflates. It looks like I've burst the bubble of whatever fantasy he had looping in his mind. Without thinking, I grab hold of his arm and squeeze it tight. A friendly type of squeeze. "You're right: tomorrow is not promised to any Fairy," I begin, "so why don't we take this one step at a time? Besides, we could be flying right into our deaths. So, what the hell?" I shrug, giving way to the flitting in my belly, the butterflies swirling in a magical cyclone of endless possibilities.

"Let's start from the beginning." I squish his hand in mine and shake vigorously. "I'm Windy, no middle name Breeze. I'm seventeen and a half, and I love my Junkyard life."

Prince Nigel's lips part in a beautiful, beguiling smile. "Lovely to meet you, Windy, no middle name Breeze. I am Prince Nigel Cloud III, but you may call me Nigel. I am nineteen, and one day I will be the ruler of Quill."

Chapter 22: Windy

Home sweet home! Or rather, home sweet Junkyard.

I'll work on that.

The carriage descends onto Junkyard soil next to the broken front door, where it looks like a struggle occurred. I'm stumbling out of the carriage, not waiting for it to fully land and fall flat on my belly. Ignoring the thrumming pain, I hurry to inspect my home for any signs of my Dad or my Dragon. The house is a wreck! Well, it's always been somewhat of a wreck in its own beautiful right, but this is different. Mister Ed must've fought tooth and nail as the kitchen and our tiny, shared living area is all scuffed up with what appear to be claw marks and deep pit marks on the floors and walls. Mister Ed probably used his cane to give the Dragonborn intruders a good walloping. Yet, as I stand amid the carnage of broken chairs, a decimated kitchen, and a streak of blood, I can only assume the worst has happened. I try to convince my heart not to break, not to crumble into a million pieces, but my heart doesn't listen. I'm breathless as a horrifying scene of Mister Ed being killed by Dragonborns blooms alive in my mind.

My only question is why? Why would Dragonborns want Mister Ed? And, if Bur'Vis is correct, what do the Dragonborns want from me?

"Windy." I jump in my skin at the sound of Nigel's voice. "I'm sorry. I didn't mean to startle you."

"It's okay." Kicking aside debris, I sit atop the lone stool unscathed by the war that had happened in my home. I palm my head in my hands, half sleepy from the carriage ride, half confused and angry as all puff. "Dad. Puff-Puff. Where are you two? I swear if they hurt the both of you, I will go berserk."

Nigel softly places a hand on my shoulder. I allow this display of affection to bring me back to the present moment. I need something to keep me grounded. The press of his warm hand against my skin is welcome and comforting.

"Any clue why your Father was attacked and kidnapped by Dragonborns?" Nigel leans his elbow on the upright part of the counter, still intact.

"No." I pinch my eyes closed. "It's all so strange to me. All of this: the Ogres, the Dragonborns. Why is this happening?" Biting my bottom lip, I take out my crystal-com and dial Mister Ed's number, hoping the Dragonborn who stole his com will answer. When the line goes dead, I break down into tears. Hot, salty tears stream from my eyes, plopping on this gaudy dress I'm still wearing.

"It'll be all right, Windy," Nigel assures, rubbing my back. "I'm here with you. We'll figure this out… somehow."

The stool I'm sitting on scraps against the floor as I rush to my bedroom to throw myself into the comfort of my bed to sleep this nightmare away. Then, halfway there, I stop in the middle of the hallway. Vision cloudy with tears, I turn and stare at the rotating pink-crystal key locked behind the glass container. The key to Madeline's heart. Could this be the key the Ogre is so desperate to have?

Pounding my fist on the glass, I curse under my breath as the glass resists my efforts. Prince Nigel moves to my side; he gasps when he sees the key and removes his dagger with such ease that it's as if he's trained for this very moment his whole life. Using the hilt of his dagger, Nigel breaks the glass with a crash in one smooth go.

"Could this be the key my Ogre Uncle needs to unlock his daughter's whereabouts?" Nigel extends eager fingers to the key and removes it from its home. He licks his lips and stares at me for a long moment. I can see it in his eyes, the question burning a hole in his head, but he's hesitant to ask it.

"You can go," I say, turning my back to him and moving

forward to my destroyed bedroom, which was the scene of a Keeper battle not too long ago. "The Fairies of Quill need you. And you need them. I'll be fine on my own."

Nigel, ever the handsy Prince, interlocks his fingers with mine. I shiver, my shoulders shuddering near my ears from his touch. Peering at him, I ask, "What do you want?"

"I'm not leaving you." He tugs at my hand, requesting I face him. I do, and he whistles a cheerful noise from his nose. "As much as it pains me to say this because all my life, all I was ever trained for was to be King, I will not abandon you in your time of need. As future King, I will ensure you and your Father are reunited. And... I'd like to see a Dragonborn for myself. I think I'll need be needing that Dragon scale, by the way. And not in such a way wherein I doubt my abilities in combat against Neven but —"

A crash booms outside of my home. The Unicorn, Lady Donna, brays her alarm as the sound of her hooves beat at the scrap metal in the yard. Nigel and I scurry to the entrance, falling atop one another to inspect the noise. Crossing the threshold leading outside, I snatch a broken stool leg in my hand.

Nigel hisses in pain and uses a single hand to block out the forever sun creeping over the mountains of junk. "Stars," he yelps, "I'm burning! Is this a Dragonborn curse?"

"No, it's the sun," I shout, brushing past him to search my Junkyard for the ruckus—a skittering, banging nose that, in hindsight, can only belong to one being. "Get back inside. You'll need some sunscreen before coming out."

"I must protect you from those Dragonborn hooligans." Nigel slinks back into the house, one hand fisted, the other holding firm to his dagger.

"It's fine," I shout over my shoulder at him. "It's only..."

Just as I suspected. Tinker comes darting right for me. Her large compound eyes, flowing with greens and blues, knocks me to my backside. The Dragonfly buzzes frantically, her wings beating exhaustingly, swirling dust and dirt.

"Tinker," I bellow, using my elbows to sit up. "Calm down and tell me what's wrong?" I touch my hand to Tinker's frons and hum to her, soothing her with a song Mister Ed would sing to me whenever I awoke from a Keeper-infested nightmare, screaming my throat raw. Mister Ed was always at my bedside to calm me down with this song. He'd hum it, like I am right now, low and soft.

Tinker's vibrating wings, going a million wing beats a second, slow to a gentle flutter.

"Now tell me," I say, pressing my cheek to her frons, "what's wrong?"

I'm not sure why or how I can understand Tinker. She is a Dragonfly, and I am a mere Fairy. Still, somehow, someway, I can interpret every buzz, wing-flap, jittery movement. My mind flickers alive with imagery, a curious happening I've grown accustomed to when Tinker and I talk. Through Tinker's compound eyes, I view the Realm as she does and get a glimpse at her life, however brief it is.

Shapes and figures sway with motion in a mix of orange and ultraviolet colors. There are three figures, two with curling horns standing above a prone figure. A fourth form comes darting out, wings nearly filling my mindscape, wielding something in their hands, trying to fend off the two imposing horned devils. Tinker breaks the connection as a third Dragonborn comes into view, another with matching horns.

"There's three of them?" I gasp, horrified that my Dad is surrounded by three Dragonborns. "Take me to Mister Ed! Please, Tinker! He needs my help." Tinker lowers to the ground as I leap on her back, prepared to take flight when Prince Nigel sprints for me.

A virgin to the forever sun, the Prince is drooling at the mouth, overcome with near heatstroke. "W-Wait. Where are you going?"

"Do you have a death wish?" I shout, annoyed at him. "You've got to take it easy in the sun, or you'll die. Your body isn't used to it yet."

"I-I've noticed that now." Nigel doubles over, panting breathlessly. "I'm right behind you. A-and... I-I didn't know you spoke Dragonfly. T-That's so-so im-impressive."

"Get your tush in that carriage before you die, Prince Nigel!"

"Yes, ma'am!"

"Tinker!" I roar, patting her atop her head, where her blind spot is. "Let's goooooo!"

***

Tinker is soaring so fast through the forever sunny skies that I loop my arms around her neck and hold tight. I shut my eyes against the golden glare of the sun, baking my skin as Tinker goes higher and higher, faster, and faster. Lifting my head against the gravitational force is a no-go. The pressure on my body leaves me in a weakened state. I want to check and see if Nigel is on our tail, but the power that gravity has on me makes it impossible to do so.

Suddenly, the sun, bright and hot against my skin, vanishes. The heat disappears from my body, and Tinker comes to a rapid landing in an unfamiliar Realm. As far as I can see, sunflowers—blues, yellows, purples, pinks, and gold—are as tall as mountains. Their green stems plunge to a depth I can't fathom because thick, ashen clouds obstruct my view of the Realm below.

Scanning the overgrown sunflowers, my eyes widen when I notice a battle ensuing at the center of the floret. A male Fairy with peculiar amaranthine wings, clothed in golden sunflower petals, engages in a heated battle with two Dragonborns—the Dragonborns I witnessed with Amana. Breathlessly, I leap from Tinker's back and am ready to run to the fight, but Tinker nudges me with her head.

Turning to her, I fumble backward as she gestures with her abdomen to thousands of jelly-like, yellow eggs crawling with life within a hollow petal bursting with water. Tinker's panic is palpable as understanding whacks me in the noggin. "You're a mommy!" I exclaim. "And you want to protect your little ones from the Dragonborns?"

"Windy!" Nigel and Lady Donna come to a near crash landing atop a sunflower next to us. "Where are we? What is this place?" Nigel stumbles out of the carriage, a sword strapped to his back.

"We've got to protect Tinker's babies and—" I survey the sunflowers waving in a strong breeze. "And my Dad." I point to the familiar brown cloaks of Mister Ed, struggling to remove himself from the fight. "DAD!" I shout.

"W-Windy?" He says, voice a mix of fear and surprise. Mister Ed hobbles from sunflower to sunflower, leaping between the large petals, near collapsing. "You must leave this place, Windy. It is too dangerous."

"I'm not leaving without you."

In a blur of green, a Dragonborn abruptly snatches me up and up. The Dragonborn crushes me to his scaly chest, green and as hard as rocks. I peer up to look at him, to glimpse at the kidnapper responsible for this mess. The cheeky Dragonborn, with shorn blond hair and deep mahogany eyes, winks at me. His hardened claws dig into the skin of my back. I have no time to scream, though.

The Dragonborn flings me upward, ripping the back of my dress and sending me soaring into the infinite blue above.

My wings ignite to a flutter, failing at the job they were created for: flying. I'm freefalling next, begging my wings to save me. But the recent damage to my left wing leaves me spinning in circles and clawing in the air.

"I've got you!" Mister Ed—my Dad, comes to my rescue. He embraces me in a hug, stabilizing me in the air. It's been forever since I've seen my Dad's translucent, almost invisible wings. His wings are void of colors, but that doesn't mean they are any less beautiful because of it.

I pull him close to me, nearly sobbing. "I'm so sorry, Dad. I'm sorry for everything."

"It's all right, Windy," He says as we descend to a waiting sunflower. "I'm here." We land with a soft *plop*. My Dad beams at me, his face scarred by the Dragonborns claws. "I'll always be here for you. You are my light."

All at once, my Dad, Edward Breeze, the Fairy who told me I would never know darkness again, slips from my arms. Blood dribbles from his mouth, his body quivering as claws spear through his backside, then retract with a sickening squish.

"NO!" Everything moves in slow motion. His body goes limp. The smile on his face withers away. His hands reach for me as he falls between the gaps in the sunflowers.

I'm diving for him, to save him. The only Fairy I've ever loved. My Dad.

It's only when I am falling that I quickly remember I cannot fly.

Chapter 23: Nigel

It all happens so fast that I don't have time to react. All I can do is watch and stare helplessly as Windy is taken to heights sure to cause asphyxiation. What future King am I if I cannot save the Fairy I have eyes for? I shake my wings free and leap in the air. I'm climbing upward to save Windy as a flaming ball of fire zips past me. I'd be toast had I not jerked to the right in time.

"And who do I have the pleasure of killing today?" A Dragonborn grins at me. His teeth serrated, yellowed, and stained with blood. This Dragonborn is about my height, wholly covered in emerald scales that appear more like armor than skin, as his face is scale-free. His wings, gloriously spread wide, are the length of two of me, and I am a rather tall Prince. Curly blond hair frames his sharp, devious face.

His reddish-brown eyes peruse my clothing. "My, my. You're a royal," he hisses, forked tongue darting at me. "Do you know how much money I could collect from a lock of your hair alone?"

"Save it." I unsheathe my sword—well, more appropriately, Mikah's sword.

"How splendid," the Dragonborn cheers. "Let's see what you're made of."

"Don't!" a voice comes from behind me. "It would be death for you, Prince Nigel. It's not worth it."

I glance over my shoulder at the Fairy with pinkish wings fluttering several feet behind me. This Fairy is familiar. His face is one I know but cannot put a name to at this moment. Nestled under his arm, a balloon-shaped Dragon sticks his tongue out at me.

My heart breaks as I hear Windy scream, "NO!"

"Seems as if our job is done," the Dragonborn says, clapping their clawed hands together. "Brother." He sighs, pointing at the Fairy—no, the balloon Dragon. "We are eager to devour the heart of the one you love, Too-da-loo." The Dragonborn dissipates in a Puff of green smoke into the ether.

Windy is falling next to save her Father as he plummets between the sunflowers and into the electric storm burning brightly in the clouds.

"Catch," the Fairy says, tossing me the tiny Dragon. I catch the Dragon in my arms, and the creature stares at me crossed-eyed. The pink-winged Fairy hurtles after Windy and her Father, his wings stirring up a whirlwind from which I turn my head as it causes my eyes to water.

The second Dragon-born shoots to my side, a single claw bathed in blood. "Brother," he says to the baby Dragon in my arms. "It is time to bring this to an end. I've had my fun." His ruby eyes find mine. "Nasturtium will soon fall. All you Fairies must pay for the sins of your ancestors. You Fairies are monsters, destroyers of Realms. I'm not one for history, but I should've done my due diligence and done better research before coming here. I wondered why the Cosmic Gods locked Nasturtium's portals. It's because of you Fairies. The Gods did their best to contain the plague before the infection spread."

"What the hell are you talking about?" I have no words to speak to this abomination who took the life of another Fairy. "You're a monster, a murderer. You killed an innocent Fairy in cold blood. I will enact my revenge—"

"Save it, royal pants." He sneers, garnet eyes like fire. "Do you know who that Fairy is? Have you no clue what he's done to our kind? To *my* family? Answer me this if you can: do you know who *you* truly are? What *you* truly are? The Storytellers have made you new-age Fairies weak! They've wiped clean the Fairy origins from your young, unsuspecting eyes." The Dragonborn shakes his head, baffled. "Now, Brother, your hex will be temporarily unwound for you to remember who you truly are."

He's speaking to the baby Dragon again. "This world is not for *our* kind to dwell in for far too long. Hurry along and finish your task so that we may drink ourselves skunk-mad in celebration. See you soon, Leopoldo the wyrm."

The talkative Dragonborn vanishes, and my arms grow heavy as the Dragon glows with a light so bright I shut my eyes. When I open them, I am startled to find a nude Dragonborn male swaddled in my arms.

"Stars!" I shout as I release my hold to send the Dragonborn sailing to the sunflowers below. The Dragonborn expands his wings, circles in the air before reaching a safe landing beside Tinker, who presses her enormous eyes against his green chest. It occurs to me that *that* baby Dragon was Windy's pet, and he evolved into a fully grown Dragonborn male.

I have no time to process my confusion as the Pink-winged Fairy calls for me. "I need help, Prince Nigel. These two are banged up—"

I'm swooping in to give a helping hand before he can finish his sentence.

The storm thrashing beneath the multitude of sunflowers jostles the florae to near tipping over. Riveted by this wonderland of girasoles, I peek between the yellow petals beneath me. The lightning flashes deathly streaks of vibrant blue and rocks the flower I am on.

"Careful," the pink-winged Fairy, whose name I have yet to ask, sits cross-legged beside an unconscious Windy and her Father. Windy's blue hair is fanned all around her, her face twitching, fingers curling as a dream enters her mind. Her Father is worse for wear: bruises well on his head, and his wounds, open and oozing, are too nauseating to look at.

"I wouldn't want you to fall, Prince Nigel," the mysterious Fairy says.

"How do you…" I begin to ask, then stop mid-sentence. The pink-winged Fairy cups a bowl of petals in his hand and uses his fingers to mix a powdery, white mixture. He blows on the mixture. A dusting of white, like snowflakes, sprinkles on the faces of Windy and her Father. The Fairy then waves a hand along the length of the elder Fairy's torn abdomen. Like some sort of magician, using a magic unknown, the pink-winged Fairy seals the wounds afflicting the elder Fairy. I observe the mysterious Fairy's features, perfect posture, and wings. This Fairy shares a resemblance to: "Matriarch Xenobia?" I say aloud.

"Ha," the Fairy laughs. "I would've been Patriarch Xenobia had I stayed."

"Y-you're Maestro!" I leap to my feet, startled that I've found the missing Prince. "The heir to the Zepyterian throne. I-I remember hearing something about you abandoning your Realm because you couldn't manage the weight of being a royal."

Maestro works his jaw, grinding his teeth. He sets the bowl aside and drifts to his feet. Palming his bald head, Maestro glowers at me as if I am the cause of all his problems. "I remember when I had that innocence—that *blissful* ignorance." He swims in the air until he's hovering a few inches over the sunflower. "Has King Nigel II told you anything? How old are you? Sixteen? Seventeen?"

"I'm nineteen!" I correct.

"And you still have no clue about the truth?" His light orange eyes inspect me, then glide to the nude Dragonborn male, marching away from Tinker toward us. "Why are you still here?"

"Is Windy all right?" the Dragonborn, Leopoldo, asks. He goes to squat near Windy, but I'm hurriedly shoving him aside. "What are you doing?"

"Don't touch her. And please, for the love of Stars, cover your bits." I tend to Windy, lifting her head in my hands.

"I've been gracious enough to allow you to stay here long enough," Maestro says to Leopoldo, folding his arms. "Had this Fairy—" He gesticulates with his jaw to Windy's Father. "—been in his prime, he would've slain you and your brethren. Have you no wits about you, Dragonborn?"

Leopoldo shrugs. "My brain is still fogged from being hexed." He sweeps a hand through his long, blond hair. "I vaguely recognize him..." His red-brown eyes then go wide in knowing. "Well, I'll be. Stepmother must have known what she was doing to send me to him. Perhaps she positioned me in a way as to spy on this executioner and destroyer of holy matrimony. That Fairy goes by Edward Breeze in this realm, but his real name is—" Leopoldo drops on his hands and knees in a heap, convulses, and in a flash of white, he's transformed back into that balloon Dragon.

Tongue lolling, muzzle twitching, Leopoldo yawns and curls up beside Windy.

I quiver, truly disturbed. "That's... creepy."

Maestro lands on his feet and beckons me to his side. "Prince Nigel, what has your Father relayed to you about Nasturtium?"

"Well," I start, scratching my cheek, "a bunch of nothing. Then I met my Uncle, and he's... he's..." I can't even speak the words.

"An Ogre." Maestro doesn't even bat an eye when he says it. I want to ask how he knows so much, but I don't because I feel this former royal is about to fill me in. "Prince Nigel, you were supposed to have the talk on your sixteenth birthday."

"Like the birds and the bees kind of talk?" I snort, but Maestro doesn't find that amusing.

"All the royals of each Realm are tasked to relay vital information to their descendants," He says as we walk side by side, shoulder to shoulder. "The royals of Zepyteria, Quill, Crest, Abethia, and Luxon are the Storytellers—the writers of history. As a royal, you must work in tandem with the royals from each Realm to sway all Fairies in a way that suits the whole of Nasturtium. However, to become a Storyteller, you must swear an oath by drinking the blood of a Human."

Maestro strides ahead, leaving me behind in my unnerved dysphoria. "Storytellers? The blood of a Human... Maestro, I feel as if I am losing my sanity."

Maestro whips around to face me. "When the truth was revealed to me, I thought it was but a fable. Until my parents took my sister and me to the Deep—the Human lair."

"Why are there Humans in Nasturtium?"

"Our Fairy forefathers enslaved Humankind when they realized the effects Human blood had on a Fairies." Maestro unveils a vial like the one I saw Father wield at the Kingdom. "I've had this with me since my first and last visit to the Deep. This vial holds enough Human blood to empower me with magic beyond anything I can understand. This blood would've been the deciding factor in that bout you witnessed with the Dragonborns had I dared to imbibe the potion. But for a year, I would be consumed by the aftereffects. Human blood is so addictive that royals from all Realms must keep a trained eye on the Human population. Their collective fear is that some royal may steal away a few Humans to become likened to that of a God. But the side aftereffects are... gruesome."

"I need to sit down." I drop to my knees and shove my head into the palms of my hands. "May I ask, does Nasturtium belong to Ogres? If so, where are we Fairies from? Where is our true home?"

Maestro's wings flutter to a slow, tender beat. "Nasturtium, long ago, once belonged to Ogres. We Fairies are invaders—non-natives—who've overthrown, murdered, and erased that of the rich Ogre history. I don't recall the name of the *true* Fairy home as it was lost long ago because of the constant Realm-hopping, if you will."

"Why would our kind invade this Realm to murder the native Ogres?" My heart becomes heavy, filled to the brim with an ice-cold sensation that forces me to gasp for air. "What are *we*?"

"Our Fairy ancestors were murderers, pillagers, kidnappers, destroyers of realms. We are the embodiment of evil."

"That can't be true," I protest, waving my hands. "What about all the wonders we've created? From the books written by scholars. To the foods passed down through the generations. We have crafted marvelous wonders and made great strides in the technological advancement of our species? You cannot deny there is goodness within Fairy kind." I turn to gaze at Windy, sleeping soundly. My heart pulsating a song of hope. "What about love?"

Maestro takes into consideration everything I've laid out for him. "All of that comes with being trapped in Nasturtium. We are caged here, like the animals we are, deservedly so. With the entrapment comes the loss of who we are. Aside from the royals who know the truth, who hide it from the everyday Fairy, the commoner has no wits about who they truly are. And thus, yes, most Fairy kind have become much more... pleasant over the many generations. But the core of who we are cannot be altered."

"What if we kept it that way? What if we kept every Fairy-kind blind to the truth? What if I—"

"The truth will, one day, be revealed to all," Maestro sighs, wiping a thumb across his eyebrow, glistening sweat. "The veil of lies will soon burn to ash, and the end of our kind will eventually come to pass. These Realms have cared for us for far too long—a parasite leeching vital nutrients soon to be extracted. Annihilated."

Clutching my shirt, I grind my teeth. "How do we stop this?"

"You can't. And I think it's best if all Fairy kind is washed away for good."

"No!" My voice, a monstrous crescendo, trembles the sunflower's petals below. "No! No! No!"

Maestro frowns at me. "Prince Nigel, I admire your—"

"I will be the change Nasturtium needs. I will right this wrong."

Maestro shakes his head at me. "I thought as you did, once," he says, "but with maturity comes wisdom when I realized how little change I can influence upon the Realms. I once possessed the same will and determination you have now. However, Nasturtium belongs to Ogres and will belong to them after we perish."

"Maybe," I begin, voice shaky. "Maybe I can talk to my Uncle, Neven. He may have a solution."

"He does," Maestro says. "The question is whether he will share his knowledge with you. You're a good kid, Prince Nigel. You remind me so much of myself. Since you and your girlfriend are here, I can surmise that you two are on some quest for Neven?"

I don't even flinch when he mentions Windy being my girlfriend, and I don't feel the need to correct him. "Y-yes." I nod. "My intentions were to join Windy as she secured a key of some sort and to slay a Dragonborn and relieve him of his scales so I may defeat my Uncle. Now, though, I don't think slaying my Uncle will result in anything worthwhile if what you're telling me is true." I pat the crystal key in my pant pocket.

"I have no reason to lie, Prince Nigel." Maestro taps me on my shoulder, his head swinging left and right. "Some Fairy is here. Be on your guard. You must take Windy with you," Maestro says. "Now! Head back to Quill before it's too late. I think Neven has bitten off more than he can chew."

"What's happening?" I draw my dagger, searching this sunflower Realm for the intruder.

"My sister has come to pay me a visit!"

A crystalline carriage, hauled by a horde of unicorns, breaks through the medley of sunflowers petals, scattering fronds like a whirlwind.

Matriarch Xenobia has arrived.

Chapter 24: Nigel

"Wake up, Windy," I say frantically as I toss her over my shoulders. I should've practiced more pushups and sit-ups for better strength. Windy's extra weight pressed against me proves I slack off more than I should with calisthenics. I'll curse myself later. Right now, I must return to the carriage in one piece.

Matriarch Xenobia's royal glimmering carriage is trailed by Keepers with their swords drawn, gleaming with the vow of death. I wonder how she found us, curious about how she escaped the Kingdom and if that means Neven is dead. I've heard tales about Matriarch Xenobia and how cunning she is. How she is a royal who will have all she desires. It seems as if she desires Windy and me right this very moment.

"Prince Nigel!" Matriarch Xenobia breaks free of her carriage in a sleeveless, black ballgown that swells around her flying form. Her wings are glorious, pink, and humming a destructive promise. "Hand over the key, and I shall spare you and that girl."

I should've guessed she would want the key, presumably to keep Neven away from the daughter they share. If Neven is dead, as I presume, why would the Matriarch find the need to hunt us down? Perhaps this key unlocks more than the hiding place of the Matriarch's secret daughter?

"Go, Prince Nigel." Maestro blows his breath on the sunflower's petals, where Windy's Father is down for the count. The petals give a twitch, then it closes around the comatose Fairy. "Complete the quest Neven sent you on. Give him the key, and maybe he'll offer you a way to save Fairy-kind. I believe in you, Prince Nigel."

Maestro lifts off in a flash of pink and comes face to face with his sister. "Jordana, it's been a while."

"I have nothing to say to you," Matriarch Xenobia spits. She attempts to glide around him, but he grips her wrist to stop her. "Still foolishly and hopelessly lost, I see. Mother and Father were right about you: you're weak, unfit to rule. It is why they abandoned all hope for you."

"Because I refused to be a monster?" Maestro asks. "Because I refused to drink the blood of innocent Humans? Or was it because I refused to follow the script of the Storytellers? To follow the script that you appear to have strayed from, Jordana! I made my own way, and you can too."

"And look at all you've accomplished by forging a way on your lonesome." Matriarch Xenobia scoffs, fierce eyes casting down upon her brother. "Nothing." The Matriarch grins at her brother, and from this far, I notice her red-stained lips are dripping. "You've made a terrible mistake." Wrenching her wrist free, the Matriarch snaps Maestro's arm in two so fast that his scream comes seconds too late.

With my free hand, I yank the carriage door open and guide Windy inside, laying her flat on the seat. Slamming the door shut, I sloppily enter the kingdom's coordinates, and Lady Donna takes off the next instant. For a few freeing minutes, I let my body relax in the comfort of the seats, hoping we have got a good head start.

But when I glimpse the view outside as we lower to the vibrant green towers that are the stalks of the sunflowers, I realize we are not alone. Beneath the sunflowers, fifteen or twenty crystal carriages full of Keepers drift aloft. Waiting. When a Keeper spots my carriage, a rush of war cries charges the thunderous sky.

Lady Donna snorts as her equine form dives beneath the awaiting clouds raging with a blue-white glow.

The carriage judders, and a slash of blue lighting bursts from all sides, and I am blinded. My vision is littered with black spots. I rub my eyes, cursing when the back of the carriage is struck from behind and flips to the left. Jostled, my head collides with the carriage door. I watch helplessly as Windy's unconscious body slips across the seat before tumbling into mine. Her head against my chest, I can feel her breath's slow ebb and flow against my arm as I pull her close. The door holding both our weights creaks. The glass beneath us sighs from the pressure. I hold my breath, press Windy closer to me.

Above, a carriage of Keepers lowers to the door directly above me. A Keeper jumps from their carriage, black wings spread wide, sword angled downward. The Keeper is mere centimeters from plunging through the window, sword shimmering in the lighting. Suddenly, the carriage rights itself, and the Keeper is knocked away. I fall atop Windy and choke out a hysterical laugh as her eyes pop open.

"What the Puff are you doing?" Windy shoves me away and sits up on her knees. Rubbing her head, she gawks at the events surrounding us.

"Y-You're okay!" I sweep her ropes of hair over her shoulder.

"What's going on?" She backs into me, her nostrils flaring. "Why are there Keepers following us—"

A Keeper's sword punctures the top of the carriage, a hair away from Windy's head. I yank her into me, her body shaking in fear. The sword vanishes into the slit it made, and through it, rainwater flows freely inside. The blade appears again and again and again, ripping the top to shreds.

"I must protect you," I whisper against her hair. "Takes this." I slip the key into the palms of her hands. Windy takes it and nods her head. "I hope against hope that Neven is alive. If he is, give this to him and go with him. I can't believe I'm going to say this, but you'll be safer with the Ogres. If Neven is dead... you've got to run and never look back."

Windy hugs me tight. Desperately. "Y-You don't have to fight. We can run—"

An explosion of thunder cuts her off and shakes the carriage and the sword-happy Keeper from atop.

Windy's hopeful brown eyes swell with tears. I wipe my thumb across her wet cheeks and smile at her. If this weren't a life-or-death situation, where Lady Donna is working her tail off to deliver us to my home through this storm, I'd stay here all day and stare at Windy's beautiful face. I hate to see a lady cry in my presence.

I am Prince Nigel of Quill, I remind myself. I cannot and will not allow any harm to come to this precious Fairy snuggled in my arms.

I slowly unlink my arms from around Windy, our eyes joined in a dance. Windy slowly glides her hands to the sides of my face, stiffened with fear but gently eases into relaxation. Windy guides my mouth to hers. Our lips meet. Heat consuming me, lulling me into a deep need. A violent want.

"What was that for?" I whisper against the raging storm and the Keepers' battle cry.

Windy shrugs. Her brown cheeks tickled with cherry. "A just-in-case kiss."

"Just in case I don't survive."

Windy nods.

"Have you no faith in me?"

"I'm scared, is all."

"Don't be," I say, brushing my nose against hers. "I will not fail you."

I spin away from her, kick open the carriage door, and take off to defend this wonderful Fairy who has burrowed herself into my heart like a hare seeking shelter.

Aloft in the darkened clouds, sword prepared to siphon the life from my attackers, flashes of lightning reflect off the silvery armor of the Keeper-horde. I am a songbird walled in by a cast of falcons.

"Give us the key," the Keepers say altogether.

"No."

My protest is met with a Keeper diving for me, his sword hissing through the air, aiming to slit my throat. I parry his attack, and our weapons clash—metal on metal ringing through my bones. Gliding away, I whirl around as another Keeper lunges for me, sword arching to cut me down. I evade his attack, his blade moving faster than the eye. That was too close for comfort.

The Keepers begin to bridge the gap—moving like wraiths poised to drag me to my doom. Suddenly, I am surrounded by the iron-clad protectors of Zepyteria, their wings mimicking the thunderous clamor of the storm. I take wing, climbing upward through the darkened grey mist, exploding into the sunflower world higher up. The Keepers zip behind me, armor clattering.

All I need to do is keep the Keepers away from Windy—

My world explodes into stars by a punch to my head that sends me spiraling into the heart of a sunflowers disk floret. Mikah's sword sails out of my grip. Matriarch Xenobia looms over me through my star-filled haze, wicked and hauntingly vile. As if controlled by an unseen force, my body is lifted upward by a swirling pink mass created by the Matriarch's hand. The "hand" caresses my body, seeking, searching for the—

"Windy has the key," Matriarch Xenobia announces, her voice booming. "Kill the girl and retrieve the key." The monarch's loyal Keepers obey as they plunge back toward the carriage.

"No!" My efforts to stand are met with defeat. The Matriarch's magic binds me to the sunflower. "D-Don't hurt her."

Matriarch Xenobia's eyes, fringed with coal eyeliner, widen in recognition. She guffaws. "You *like* Windy? I am severely disappointed in you, Prince Nigel. Of all the garlands available for you to choose from, you've grown to like that creature soon to meet her death."

"Windy is not a creature." I wish to say those words to the she-devil, but they do not come from my mouth.

Leopoldo. He descends next to me, nude body an unwanted distraction. "Call off your men, and I shall spare your life."

"A Dragonborn," Matriarch Xenobia's magical grip falters, waning out. I take this distraction to stagger to my feet and seek out Mikah's wayward sword. "I had thought we Fairies had seen the last of you beasts. Yet, here you are in the flesh; it's a most delicious sight. Although my mind is riddled with questions, I must be off."

"Jordana!" Maestro emerges out of thin air like a magician, a glittering veil of blue sweeping around him as the royal materializes. A red streak of blood at the corner of Maestro's mouth tells me he's possessed by the Human elixir he had saved since his youth. "It is time to bring your rein to an end."

"Is it now?" Matriarch Xenobia flutters her eyelashes coyly, threateningly.

"Nigel, Leopoldo, I've got it from here." The siblings vanish and reappear seconds later, engaged in an epic aerial battle. Magic against magic. Pinks clashing with blues, painting the heavens a bright purple.

"Come now," Leopoldo says, wings expanding like lungs overfilled with breath. "We must save the love of my life."

I hesitate—a second that will cost Windy her life. "What do you mean by that?" I ask. "Do you mean in the way a dog loves its master?"

Leopoldo frowns. "I saw how you fought to protect Windy," he says, green wings humming like honeybees. "Please, heed my warning: Windy shall be mine. Should you dare touch her again, I will not hesitate to snap your neck."

Leopoldo dives between the petals, forcing me to swallow the words I have lodged in my throat. I pick up Mikah's sword lying at my feet, then plunge into the thunderstorm below.

Leopoldo is a force to be reckoned with! The Dragonborn cuts through the Keepers' armor with his sharp claws, snuffing out their life without blinking twice. His Dragon wings provide him the upper hand he needs to swim through the skies with the practiced ease of a dancer. This isn't Leopoldo's first time taking a life. I doubt it will be his last. The Dragonborn nods at me to engage the Keepers crowding the carriage.

"When did you become the leader?" I dart forward, my wings fluttering against the tumult. "I am a Prince," I shout, "I have the final say."

"I am a Prince as well, Nigel." Leopoldo's claws sink home, cracking a Keeper's helmet and piercing his skull. "We can fight about this later. Now is not—" a Keeper's sword slides against Leopold's carapace. The blade shatters like glass.

As I near the carriage barreling through the storm, angling the sword in my hand to swipe at the Keeper nearest me, a blue can of fizzy, sugary blueberry goodness explodes in the Keeper's face. The Keeper wipes at their eyes, frantic.

"Puff, yeah!"

Windy is atop the carriage, balancing for dear life. She wields one of my wooden legs in her hand like a bat and another can of bubbly drink in the other. Windy's dress is torn in an intricate but messy pattern that allows her to cradle a bevy of beverages within the folds of the fabric like a hammock.

Windy shakes a can of red bubbly—a cherry-flavored drink— furiously. Tosses the can up and strikes it with all her might. The can explodes upon contact with a creeping Keeper, his cries of surprise drowned by the raging storm. The blue-haired Fairy continues her ceaseless wrath, employing the cans of drink as improvised weapons of bubbly destruction. At the same time, I take out the unsuspecting Keepers lurking about; their surprise at Windy's ingenuity baffles them.

I render a few Keepers lifeless, their bodies spiraling away toward the Realm below.

"Nice work, Windy," I cheer as more sugar bombs detonate around me.

"Thank you." Windy pats at her dress, her features going rigid. "Crud!" She's out of ammunition. A Keeper swings to strike her, their blade pledging Windy's demise. I'm by her side, moving her out of harm's way. I thrust my blade forward; it slips through the Keeper's throat in one fluid motion. I use the last ounce of my strength to kick the Keeper off the blade, their garbled scream overpowered by the blood gurgling from their mouth. The Keeper's body falls, and mine does as well. The exhaustion of battle taking its toll on me.

Windy grabs hold of me before I teeter off the edge.

"Prince Nigel," she cries, "are you okay—"

Another explosion sounds. This one is not followed by the sweet taste of sugar but by the bite of copper on my tongue and the kiss of darkness consuming me whole. The last thing I remember is a surging vivid pink sphere rushing towards us and Windy's terrified scream as the carriage disintegrated into ash.

Chapter 25: Windy

I don't recall much after that pinkish light exploded, and the carriage melted to nothingness. All I remember is falling down, down, down, and the shimmering, gold earth below rushing to meet me. A pair of wings had swaddled around me like a blanket as my ears filled with monstrous explosions booming everywhere.

I am alive, greeted by an endless Realm of sand, the blazing, forever sun shining on me, and an unconscious Prince at my side. We are in the Gnobi desert, an all-encompassing dust bowl that meets the border of every Realm. This desert's sun will be the death of us. I've got to find a shaded area. But there's nothing but miles upon miles of glittering sand in all directions.

My mouth goes dry from the anxiety nipping away at me. Puff… I should've saved a few cans of fizzy drink. I exhale as a yip comes from under the Prince.

"Puff-Puff?" I say, brows raised. Rolling the very heavy Prince Nigel to his side, I am met with that cute grin that is my balloon Dragon. "Puff-Puff." I squeeze him tight in my arms and shower him with kisses. "I'm sorry, bud, but I think this is how we die."

Puff-Puff coos. I don't think my littlest Dragon understands the danger we are in, and that's okay. Puff-Puff isn't the most intelligent creature, but his cuteness makes up for it. My balloon Dragon tugs at my dress, chewing on something trying to wiggle itself free.

It's the key!

I unearth the key from the many folds of my dress and hold tight to it. The key is moving on its own like magic. The pink key tugs me with such force I must leap to my feet or be dragged by it. This thing has a mind of its own. And it's leading me somewhere... like a compass.

"Puff-Puff," I say, feet gliding in the sand. "I need you to be a big Dragon and help move the Prince's body. Can you do that?" I grind out that last sentence. This key is trying its darndest to slip out of my grasp.

Puff-Puff sniffs Prince Nigel's hair and growls.

"Puff-Puff!" I groan. "I need your help."

My littlest Dragon pinches the hem of Prince Nigel's right pant leg between his teeth.

"Good boy," I cheer like the proud owner I am. "This way."

Whatever magic fuels this key overpowers me to the point where I nearly lose my hold on it. My brows are slick with sweat that pollutes my vision with salty droplets, and my fingers grow numb from holding tight to the key. How far will this thing drag me around the desert?

With my free hand, I've stripped away layers of my dress to give to my Dragon for him to gnaw on. With Puff-Puff's generous helping of saliva, I direct my Dragon to wrap the cloth around the Prince's neck and head. This should keep the Prince cool for a good while. However, I am unsure how long a "good while" is in relation to the sea of sand consuming everything. Worst of all, I'm starving! How's a Fairy like me supposed to think on an empty belly?

I sneak a glance at Puff-Puff and lick my lips. That lick was either out of hunger or because my lips are so darned chapped. I hope it's the latter. Eating my sweet little, plump-juicy Dragon would break my heart.

Puff-Puff looks my way, curious.

"What?" I turn my head away from him.

My balloon Dragon yips at me as if the tiny balloon creature can read my thoughts.

I laugh, "I won't eat you. I Promise."

Puff-Puff lowers his eyes to serpentine slits.

"How's our Prince doing?" I ask, using one hand to shield

my eyes from the sun.

Puff-Puff whimpers.

When I see the Prince, I bite my lower lip. Prince Nigel's entire face is as red as the innards of a blood orange. His sensitivity to being overexposed to this gnarly sun will soon kill him. There's nothing more I can do, though. After all he's done for me: coming to my rescue and saving my Puff-Puff and me from going splat, the least I can do is keep him alive.

Everything looks bleak in this never-ending sandscape until the key suddenly stops pulling me, and I collide with an invisible force. Slowly, I reach out my free hand, touching something solid but transparent enough to see the desert beyond. The key gently buzzes in my hand: a rapid-fire buzz telling me when I am hot and a soft pulsating beat when I'm cold. This magical thing is guiding me to—

Something like a lock clicks open. All at once, the transparent thing becomes a home—a hut crafted entirely of sand.

The door to the hut swings open.

"Jordanna, I was getting worried—"

That deep earth skin. Those spiraling curls. And those leafy green eyes illuminated by dawning sunlight.

"Madeline..." I hadn't thought I would see her, hadn't expected to meet her in the middle of the Gnobi desert, of all places. Judging by her startled face and wide eyes, the feeling is mutual. I'm unsure why, but I pull her close in a desperate embrace. "Mom," I say and, despite myself, I cannot hold in the cry of joy that escapes me.

"W-Windy?" She whispers my name as her arms go stiff at her sides.

"Mommy?" A squeaky voice comes from behind Madeline. "Who is that?"

I open my wet eyes and see an olive-skinned Fairy with cat-shaped amaranthine eyes and a face much like the Matriarch Xenobia's. The Fairy's stick-thin figure is engulfed in a cerulean dress she wears. Her hair, shaded a dirty blonde color, is matted on the side of her head. I guess having a Matriarch for a mother doesn't come with the amenities of looking put together.

"Go back to your room, Abby," Madeline says, removing my arms from around her. "Please."

Abby shakes her head. "No."

"Go back to your room. NOW!" Madeline wheels to face Abby, snatches the Fairy's arm and hauls her into a room. "Don't come out until our guests leave. Do you understand me?"

"Yes, Mommy."

When Madeline faces me again, I take this fleeting time to assess her—my Mom. Madeline is disheveled, her clothing nothing but rags, and her posture slumped. It's as if Madeline has lived a thousand lives all at once in this desert domain. All of Madeline's sweetness—the sweetness I felt when she cared for me all those years ago—is burned to cinders when she opens her mouth to yell at me.

"What the hell are you doing here?" Madeline gives me a cursory glance before her eyes land on Prince Nigel. "This must be a dream. You need to go. You cannot stay here."

"So much for pleasantries," I sass back. Puff-Puff drags the Prince inside the home, then falls over panting. "If you hadn't noticed," I start, pointing at the Prince, "we need shelter and—" my stomach grumbles "—sustenance."

"You'll find nothing of the sort here," Madeline snaps. She makes a beeline for the door and gestures to the impossibly sandy Realm outside. "Leave. I'm begging you."

Prince Nigel coughs, his eyes flutter open. I step around Madeline to check on the red-faced Fairy. The royal gulps dryly and tends a shaky hand to his throat. "Water." His voice is a rasp, barely audible.

"He needs water." I stare at Madeline with pleading eyes. "Or he'll die of dehydration." My following string of words is expelled, intending to leave a bruise. "But, I'm sure you're used to seeing death and not doing anything to intervene. Watching all those servants of Namanzi die must've been worthwhile."

Madeline's lips twitch, annoyance pulling her features

into something dark and scary. Gingerly, Madeline walks forward and into an arching entryway at the back of this tiny home. She returns with a glass of water in her trembling hand and offers it to me. I take the glass and tilt the rim to the Prince's dry lips. Prince Nigel's lips form a weak smile as he finishes.

"Thank you." The Prince props himself on a wall.

"Prince Nigel," I say, my head swiveling from him to Madeline standing near the open door. "This is Madeline. My mother."

He splutters and lays a cupped hand over his mouth. "My brain hurts." He rubs his fingers at the center of his head. "Did you... did you just say she is your mother?"

"Yes," I sigh.

"I have a sister?" Abby races out of her room. "I've always wanted a sister."

"Abby!" Madeline, flustered by the unruly Fairy, takes Abby's hand. "How much did you hear?"

Abby goes still, her silence the loudest sound in existence. "Everything." Abby then implores, "Mommy said I was a servant of Namanzi. Am I going to die, too?"

Madeline falls to her knees. "No, Abby, of course not." She kisses the back of Abby's hand. "You misheard Windy," Madeline says, fumbling her words. "You *are* Namanzi's new body, Abby Gale. What did Mommy Jordana tell you about ascending? Huh?"

"That Gods cannot die," Abby says with practiced ease.

"Which also means?"

"I'll live forever and ever." Abby twirls in that too-large dress she's wearing.

Prince Nigel whispers to me: "Is that *her*? Neven's daughter?"

I bob my head. "That's your cousin, Prince."

Nigel clambers to his feet, wobbles, but doesn't fall. "Madeline," Nigel croaks, his voice coming and going. "I formally request that you be our escort out of this desert nightmare and back to Quill. It is urgent that my Uncle, Neven, sees his daughter, Abby."

Madeline slaps her hands over Abby's ears. The young Fairy cringes in pain. "Don't you dare speak that name to me again." Madeline glares at the Prince, nostrils flared. "Jordana and I are doing everything possible to protect *our* daughter from Neven."

"Do you honestly believe that, Madeline?" Prince Nigel mirrors my sentiments. "Matriarch Xenobia tried to kill Windy and me..." he pauses and glances at Abby's puzzled face. The Prince settles for pantomiming a knife cutting a throat with his finger. "Matriarch Xenobia is an unhinged Fairy. And you know this to be true, don't you."

"She knows," I grumble, folding my arms. "Madeline knows everything. I had hoped there was good in her. That there was an explanation behind her actions. Mom," I say hopelessly, cringing at the sound of desperation heavy in my voice, "help us. Matriarch Xenobia can't be trusted. If she is willing to hurt me—a Fairy, you, and her, secretly adopted—then she'll hurt you too."

Prince Nigel puts a hand on my shoulder. "Repeat that last part again?" He regards me questioningly. "Matriarch Xenobia adopted you?"

"Sort of." I tilt my head left and right. "Yes. It's complicated."

"That means you're a Princess." Nigel's face sparkles with admiration. "Which means you can usurp the throne from the crazy Matriarch by having her committed to a life of imprisonment for her crimes—"

"If only it were that simple."

Matriarch Xenobia's voice makes Prince Nigel and I both gasp. The Matriarch saunters inside the already crammed home, her presence suffocating. The royal's black ballgown is pattered with red and signed as if it has danced with Dragon's fire. Prince Nigel steps ahead and holds his arm before me like a protective shield. His fingers play on the edge of the hilt of his dagger.

"Mommy." Abby wiggles free of Madeline's hands and bounds for her mother. The Matriarch holds up a hand, stopping the Fairy. Abby's head falls, shoulders slumped. Poor Fairy.

"Remember when we flipped that coin, Maddy?" Matriarch Xenobia clasps her hands together and glides toward Madeline.

"Don't." Madeline shoots to her feet. She raises her hands, asking without words for the Matriarch to cease speaking. "Don't. Jordana. I love you. Don't do this."

Matriarch Xenobia pushes Madeline aside, whose face is so terror-stricken that something inside me breaks. Whatever the Matriarch is about to say, it has something to do with me.

"Come now, Maddy," Matriarch Xenobia grins. "I'm sure you remember the day we flipped that coin, oh, almost eighteen years ago. Don't you remember: heads for the baby girl or tails for the baby boy. Whichever baby fate chose, we'd adopt in secret. Whilst the other would be fed to the pack of dogs known to roam the Palace grounds."

"Enough, Jordana!" Madeline begs on her knees.

"Whatever is the matter, Maddy?" Matriarch Xenobia says assertively, curling her lips like a wicked vulpine. "Are you afraid of reliving that day fate decided that Windy should live and her brother should perish?"

"W-what?" It feels like this tiny home is closing in all around me. Squeezing me inside its sand-packed walls. This is not the time for a panic attack. I can't breathe. Clutching my chest as my legs give, my body shakes.

"You're a monster, Matriarch Xenobia," Prince Nigel spits.

"None worse than your Father, Prince Nigel," the Matriarch cackles.

"I'm sorry, Windy." I hear Madeline say over the din of Prince Nigel and the Matriarch exchanging words. My name is tossed about in the tumult, something about the Matriarch needing me this instant. "I'm so sorry."

The sound of Prince Nigel drawing his dagger exacerbates my panic. The Prince tilts his weapon's sharp edge at the Matriarch. "Should you inch any closer, I will be forced to strike. Matriarch or not."

Matriarch Xenobia swirls her fingers around. A pink,

twinkling mist of some nature pirouettes before her, meandering between her fingers and blossoming with hints of scarlet.

Madeline presses a hand to her mouth. "We swore to one another that we'd never again drink the blood of Humans. It's a cursed addiction that will be your downfall, Jordana. How could you lie to me? How could you betray my trust?"

"Easily." Matriarch Xenobia says coolly. "Now, Prince Nigel, though I'd stop at nothing from cutting your pathetic life short, Windy and I must be off." Turning, she addresses Abby. "It's time, my sweet Abby Gale—Namanzi's vessel."

"She's not ready, Jordana," Madeline shrieks.

"Plans change, my dear." The Matriarch plays with the mist above her hand. "Neven will not sleep until he gets his dirty Ogre hands on Abby. It's in my best interest to revive Nasturtium anew. Say goodbye to Windy, Prince Nigel. Unfortunately, today is her last day with breath in her body."

A sheer curtain of the Matriarch's glittering pink haze washes over me. A deluge of fire and ice overwhelming me, merging me with the miasma. My movements are restricted, fingers, toes, and limbs frozen by this creation of the Matriarch's doing.

Prince Nigel grasps for me, his fingers gliding through me as if I am becoming a ghost. As if my body is departing this plane. I cry out in heartbreak! My cries are matched with voices clamoring within this pink force, pulling me to my doom.

"Windy!" Prince Nigel swipes his hands through me, desperation eking out of him in anguished grunts.

"N-Nigel..." I manage to belt out as the Prince vanishes into thin air, and I land with a splash in a puddle beneath me.

There're astonished gasps around me. My name fills the unsettling, watery crypt I've found myself in.

"Windy?" someone says, their feet pattering against the floor slick with water and dried blood trails.

When I look up, I find Charm slipping toward me in a panic. The garland eases me to my feet and hugs me tight for some strange reason I can only think of as a hopeless hug. A hug of no noise or warmth. A hug that reveals the truth about our fate: we're about to die. I'm surrounded by garlands, their faces streaked with tears, their fancy dresses torn, and their hair bedraggled.

"Windy," Charm sobs, "I don't want to die here."

"Where is here?" I ask.

The Matriarch fills in the blank as her form materializes alongside Abby and Madeline. "The Temple of the Water Goddess Namanzi."

Chapter 26: Nigel

Matriarch Xenobia's magic not only ripped Windy from this world but also sent me well on my way back to my home: the Kingdom of Quill. I land in a heap of dead bodies on my back in the foyer of the Kingdom. My home is painted red with that of the blood of the citizens of Quill and Ogre. There're over hundreds of bodies sprawled in mounds, their vessels treated like refuse in the midden, discarded as if these Fairies of my realm had no purpose. These Fairies meant something to someone. Now they are nothing. Their stories have ended abruptly. Their souls will never find rest until I become King.

That day is today.

Despite my fatigue, the rumbling in my stomach, and my escalating anxiety, I will challenge Father for the throne and bring this—all of this—to an end.

I bow my head at the slaughtered Fairies as I pass by the piles of bodies. "I offer you all this promise: I will succeed my Father and bring light to this darkened Realm. Find your rest in the stars." Before I depart the foyer searching for Father, I disarm a deceased Knight of his sword and shield.

I try to maintain a sense of calm despite my skittering pulse bounding through me like a rabbit. However, preserving calm of any sort is a debilitating task. I'd never expected to see the day my Realm and my Fairies succumbed to such a nasty fate. My hope… my dream was to gift my dying Father with the golden—but deadly—warmth of the sun. To see Father's eyes alight with the remembrance of a Realm at peace. Of Mom.

All I want to do now is to stop Father's tyranny at any cost.

By instinct alone, I head for Father's chambers in this

unsettlingly mute Kingdom. I stop myself short, inches from Father's chamber door. Father wouldn't be seeking a respite from the carnage he caused. Taking a peaceful nap while the Kingdom falls to ash around us. My father wouldn't be in the Kingdom. He'd be... I don't know where.

A rustling comes from behind the door. Father?

I'm kicking the door in next, prepared to swing and end Father's life. But I halt in my tracks. Neven blinks at me from his spot on the floor, surrounded by a pool of blood. A servant with their back to me tends to his wounds. Neven's green skin is slashed in some areas and bruised in others. The chamber door slams behind me. I jerk around to fight, my sword shaky in my sweaty palm.

"Stand down," the Ogre says. I believe his name is Bur'Vis. He has the power of clairvoyance or something. "I told you the Prince would come, Neven."

Neven grunts, "But, my dear friend, you were wrong about so many other things. I'm beginning to doubt your abilities."

Bur'Vis frowns. "My *sight* is based on probabilities and should be heeded with—"

"I'm joking, my friend," Neven assures, a feeble smile sweeping the corners of his mouth upward. "Nephew, it is good to see you. Well, good to see you are alive. Bur'Vis had two visions about you: one where the Matriarch ended your life, and the other where you'd find your way back to the Kingdom."

"I'm fortunate the latter is true," I say, inching my way to the Ogre. The servant turns to me, a scowl on her face. "You." My features tighten at the sight of the Fairy, who thinks me a murderer.

The servant's scowl and disdain hasn't much changed since last we met under unfortunate circumstances. "I have no words for you, Nigel."

"What drama." Bur'Vis saunters over to assist the servant with tending to Neven. Bur'Vis gathers damp towels and beings to tear them into strips. The yellow-haired Ogre's head snaps to me, his eyes as black as a starless night. "Serena," he says to the servant. And then it hits me: Serena Claire, mother to Tara Claire. "If it pleases you, I must say that Prince Nigel has a good heart. His only failure is trying to appease his father. You and I know firsthand what King Nigel is wholly capable of."

"But that doesn't excuse what happened to my daughter." Serena's hands shake, and her voice goes out. Neven clasps her hands in his huge mitts. "Forgive me, Neven. I cannot breathe the same air as that monster."

"I'm sorry." It's all I can muster. It's all that can be said about what happened. I could've done more, yes. Yet, I stood idle, knowing Mikah was responsible for his crimes.

"Oh, would you look at that," Serena says, a mocking lilt to her tone, "my three years of pain and suffering over the loss of my daughter have been alleviated. All it took was a simple apology. If you'll excuse me, I must check on the other survivors."

"Please be careful." Neven lays his back against the floor-to-ceiling window and expels a sigh from his bruised lips.

"Serena, if I could please have a moment of your time." I proffer a hand to the servant, who regards me with poisonous eyes. "I… I was protecting my best friend. I believed him with my whole heart. I trusted he was telling me the truth about what happened—"

"Save it, Nigel." Serena glides to an alcove in Father's chamber where there had been a bust of him before it was removed. "I pray you never have a daughter whose innocence is stolen from her by a Fairy she thought cared about her. No is a complete sentence. It doesn't give any Fairy the right to someone's body. Tara took her life because of him…. I pray you, and that friend of yours burn for all eternity. Neven, Bur'Vis, please let me know when we shall voyage to the Hraylor mountains. I've grown quite ill of being here in this forsaken Kingdom." With that, Serena opens a door I hadn't known was in the alcove and disappears behind it.

I am momentarily silent to process the burgeoning

memories of Mikah and Tara's love affair. The unsavory incident that followed was a stain upon the Kingdom when Serena brought the case before Father. Tort law failed to protect Tara. It only protected the wealthy best friend of the Prince of Quill.

"If you're seeking your father," Neven begins, wiping a cloth along his brow, "he and his ruthless followers have gone to the Red Rooms."

I wrinkle my lips. "Why? Father isn't in any need of protection."

Neven sighs and shakes his head. "You really are one oblivious Prince. The Red Rooms are the gateway to the Deep—the lair of enslaved Humans. My brother will seek counsel with the royals of Abethia, Luxon, and Crest. Together they will figure out what to do and how to spin this bloodbath as one of Ogre design. My only hope is that I may find my daughter before the royals come up with something heinous. Since you are here with Bur'Vis and me, and Windy is not with you..." my Uncle seeks an answer from Bur'Vis. An answer he may have insight on.

I turn to Bur'Vis, whose powers are at work.

"I've tried over a million times in over a million ways," Bur'Vis says through a frown, "but Jordana has blocked my powers from exposing her whereabouts. And the whereabouts of your daughter."

"Windy and I found Abby." Neven's jaw goes slack at the mention of the name Abby. "She was in the Gnobi desert. Abby looks like you."

Neven hurriedly wipes at his face, streaked with sweat. Not sweat... tears. "Forgive me of my unmanly display. I'd hate for the Nephew who wished to spill my blood to view me as anything but weak."

I cross the chamber to sit beside my Uncle, placing my sword and shield at my feet. "You've nothing to worry about, Neven. I am not here to squabble with you. Besides, you're pretty banged up." Hugging my knees to my chest, I shut my eyes. "Abby and Windy were stolen away from me. I wish there was something I could do, but I failed." My gaze finds Bur'Vis's. "Are you able to get a lock on Windy?" When the Ogre shakes his head that he cannot, I lose all hope that Windy is alive.

"I cannot locate any of those Fairies Jordana magicked away," Bur'Vis says.

Neven's brows wrinkle. He coughs out, "Jordana must be at the Temple." He pats my hand and says with finality, "Windy is no more."

"How can you know for sure?" I bolt to my feet and pace about. My mind flapping in endless loops.

"Because I know how Jordana maintains her connection to Namanzi." Neven shifts uncomfortably on his rear. "Before Jordanna figured a way to forge a link with the Water Goddess, Fairies were sacrificed from all over the Realms to keep the waters afresh. You see, Namanzi had stayed behind for the rest of her Ogre Kin. She had wanted to ensure that all Ogres and escaping Humans were taken to a new Realm free from Fairy autocracy. Most Ogres that stayed behind waged a losing war on Fairies. Namazi fought alongside the Ogres, but in the end, as the last of the Gods left the plane, Namanzi's fate was sealed. All Gods who stayed behind would be turned to stone so as to steal away any chance of Fairy survival. When Namanzi was turned to stone, the waters dried up all across the Realm. The Goddess gave the Ogres a parting gift—infinite water."

I laugh weakly. "I had always wondered how Ogres had survived over a thousand years without water. There were theories, though."

"Theories that we Ogres drank the blood of Fairies?" Bur'Vis asks, folding his arms.

"You said it, not me." I bump Neven with my elbow. "So, need I ask why we Fairies thought sacrificial means was the way to keep the waters thriving?"

"Namanzi loathed Fairies," Neven continues, "so much in fact that a drop of Fairy blood spilled at the feet of her stone form would cause rain to trickle through the entire Realm. Namanzi was somehow still connected to Nasturtium. The Fairies have since abused that system—Namanzi's ceaseless hatred. Then

Jordana discovered a way to isolate the waters to just Zepyteria and forged a link with Namanzi."

"What a diabolical Matriarch," I seethe.

"A diabolical Matriarch of whom I loved..."

"How and why, Uncle?"

"I'm getting used to the way you say 'Uncle,'" Neven beams, cheeks high. "It's very kind of you." I smile at him, noticing how warm his demeanor is. How lively his energy is. "But to answer your question: Jordana and I fell in love when I hadn't thought love was possible for me."

"This was before I was born, mind you," Bur'Vis adds, "so I couldn't warn him beforehand."

Neven says, "Jordana had a light about her back when we met. She came to the Hraylor mountains seeking her brother, Maestro. Jordana thought we stole him away. She didn't find him there, although she came armed to the teeth, ready for war. What caught her off guard was our Ogre hospitality. Ogres had fought with Fairies for so long that, in the end, we Ogres waved our white flag and retreated. We had no use for war in our lives. Not anymore. I believed Jordana saw a semblance of peace among Ogre kind. I know deep in my heart that Jordana only wants peace. She was born into a Realm where she believed everything she had been taught... until her sixteenth birthday. That's when all the Prince and Princesses of each Realm are given the talk. Something your father did not have with you. Anyway, Jordana and I forged a pact that we would do all it took to overthrow the Storytellers and restore peace to Nasturtium. I believed in her. Believed there was hope for peace between Ogres and Fairies. But I was wrong. And it cost me a broken heart and my daughter..."

"Thank you, Neven," I say, "for sharing your story. It opens my eyes to who you are as a being and the kind of Fairy I hope to be. Do you honestly believe Fairies can quash the evil that runs through our veins? I encountered Maestro on my journey, and he told me such was an impossibility."

"Prince Nigel," Neven chuckles, "you found the lost

Prince? I had no idea your journey would lead you to him."

"I did," Bur'Vis chimes in, "sort of..."

"I have a good feeling about you," Neven says, grinning at me. "I have faith that you will find a way to overcome anything standing in your path. I have a restored hope in Fairy kind, thanks to you. You, Prince Nigel of Quill, have a heart of gold. Please don't let it become tainted."

"We must be off," Bur'Vis warns, his pointed ears perking up. "A feeling of... dread has shaken me to my core. Let us return to the Hraylor mountains with our new guests." Bur'Vis approaches the alcove, presses his hand on the wall, and the door swings open.

"I'll accompany you two." I begin when Neven taps me on my shoulder.

"I think you should seek out your father," Neven suggests. "King Nigel will be awaiting your return. You deserve to have all your questions answered. And—" Neven regards the discarded sword and shield with a flourish of his hand "—you came seeking to have your pressing questions have light shed upon them." My Uncle, the Ogre I once held spite in my heart for, unearths a marble from his pocket. A crystalline ball striped with gold and white, no bigger than my thumb. "Although I've lost hope of seeing my daughter, I haven't lost hope in peace. This was to be Windy's gift, but it now belongs to you. Please keep it safe."

"What is it?" I ask, peering at the pellet of glass.

Neven's answer is unheard as the Kingdom in its entirety trembles like a cold Fairy enveloped in winter's breath. Neven and Bur'Vis nod their goodbyes, leaving me to investigate the source of the disturbance on my lonesome.

Chapter 27: Nigel

The winding hall to the Red Rooms looms before me, a curving spine stretching nearly a mile long. In my younger years, whilst playing hide and seek with Mikah and a few others, I had hidden in one of the Red Rooms, knowing that no one but Father and I could gain access. I recall groaning, imperceptible screeching noises when I had crouched under a side table. I had deduced those sounds emanated from the wooden floors settling beneath me. The Red Rooms are the eldest part of the Kingdom, constructed before the Kingdom took shape.

Strange, now that I think about it.

A deteriorating red carpet leads the way down as I charge onward. As I draw near, a flickering ember glow spills from a crack in the door. Of the four doors surrounding, this central door must be where Father has departed to. Palming the door open, I am met with a commotion that dies to a quiet when I enter.

Mikah stands tall, sword in hand, blood smeared across his chin and upper body. This room has been turned inside out. Books ripped from a bookshelf, now split down the middle, are strewn across the floor. The crystal chandelier has devolved into fragments, and a flame from the overturned hearth has snaked up the sheer curtains.

Mikah gives me a once-over, barely registering my presence. "Show me where the door to the Human lair is, Nigel."

"I'm in the same boat as you are, Mikah." I tighten my fingers on the hilt of the sword, anxious. "Perhaps the entryway to the Deep is within another Red Room?"

"Damn it!" Mikah spins to the nearest wall and punches it,

his knuckles raw and bleeding. "I must get my hands on Human blood. It's the only way I'll be strong enough to rule this Realm."

"You have no idea the monster Human blood is." I keep my shield of stars and a full moon protecting my front, should Mikah see it fit to strike me unprovoked. My confidence in him has been abolished since he spat those words that my Kingdom may fall at his hands. The Fairy who stands before me is someone I don't know.

"Neither do you, Nigel."

The flames bloom marigold and ruby as it eats away at the curtains and births smaller sparks of fire on the abandoned books.

"We must leave." On instinct and memories past, I sheath my sword and extend my hand to Mikah.

Wrong move.

Mikah charges me, his skull connecting with my mouth. My mouth burns hot with the taste of blood as I stumble for balance.

"Knights of Quill," Mikah calls out, "I found Prince Nigel."

The creak of the other Red Room doors begins to open and slam shut. Knights file into the room of smoke and fire, swords drawn.

"Prince Nigel, here is our meal ticket." Mikah tosses aside my shield; it clatters to the floor. "King Nigel wouldn't want anything to happen to his little boy, now, would he?"

"Commander," one of the Knights says, "we found a panel in the other room. It appears to be an entryway but doesn't react to our touch."

"Good work, Xavi."

"Also," Xavi says as he gestures to the open door. "We found this garland."

A tangle of black hair hides the face I know belongs to Rhyanna. "Unhand me, you brute. Prince Nigel?" She tries to move to my side, but she is blocked. "What did you do, Mikah Prue?" There is a knowing exchange of a story I can't firmly grasp. All I know is, from that said exchange... Mikah and

Rhyanna know each other. But how?

"I'm going off script." Mikah shrugs. "Just like that bat-piss crazy Matriarch, I'm taking my destiny into my own hands. Show me this panel, Xavi."

Xavi leads the group as I am forcibly dragged like cattle to the butcher into the adjacent Red Room. Mikah struts a most winning strut to a gray panel inlaid beside a bookshelf that has been shoved aside. The panel shines with a golden, ancient Fairy symbology of right angles, shapes, and nonsensical swirls.

"Bring Nigel here!" Mikah orders.

I'm stood up like a mannequin to be put on display in a shop and hauled to the panel.

"Apparently," Mikah starts, his eyes going from right to left as if he's reading the symbols, "this thing only responds to those with royalty running through their veins. Lucky us, right?"

"Yes, Commander," the Knights echo.

Mikah snatches my hand in his iron grip. He mashes my hand onto the panel, and everything goes cold. My sight is impregnated with flashing images of royal's past and all those who've traversed to the Deep. The entire Cloud lineage has peered behind these walls, drank the blood of Humans, and forged contractual bonds with royals from all over Nasturtium. The last fleeting image I see is of Father and a horde of others blinking like lights out of this room and into the lair beyond.

When my eyes reset and the world rights itself, I am startled by my new surroundings. I've arrived in a starlit-infused, cavernous, rocky domain that goes on for miles and miles in all directions. The smells of sulfur and death hang heavy around me like a coat of armor. The Knights share surprised expressions; Mikah licks his lips, and Rhyanna struts ahead as if she is familiar with this dimension. Further along, through an archway of stone, a Fairy clothed in robes waits at the entry point. My Father.

Father summons the lot of us forward. "My son, I knew you'd make it. Come now. It's time for us to have ourselves a chat."

"Negative, King Nigel." Mikah pops his neck, cracks his knuckles then motions for two of his Knights to join his side. The steel kiss of Mikah's sword presses along the tender skin of my throat. "King Nigel, you abomination," Mikah snarls a wolfish noise, "I demand that you surrender the Kingdom of Quill and your precious Humans to me. Or your little boy will meet his maker."

I'm too petrified to swallow; the sword nicks my skin like a tick drawing precious blood.

"Mikah," Father says, clapping, "how fiendish of you! I grow impressed with you more and more. You remind me of our Fairy ancestors long ago. They'd stop at nothing to get what they desired. Even if that meant killing one of their own. Unfortunately, Mikah, you are breaking your code—writing a story that shouldn't exist. Are you betraying me? Are you betraying the Storytellers?"

"I make my own rules," Mikah barks. "Besides, you royals lied to our faces about the history of Nasturtium. This was once an Ogre dwelling hole before we invaded—am I correct, King?" Father nods. "For that deception alone, I reserve the right to revoke my dealings with you Storytellers. I was but a babe when I was indoctrinated and forced fed a history that never was. You royals manipulated us, the Weavers, feeding us lies daily so that we may continue to write whatever story you saw fit to tell. But enough talk, hand over your Kingdom, or Nigel, here, loses his friggin' head."

Father's lips curl into a clownish smile. "Rhyanna, have you betrayed me as well?"

Rhyanna's jaw ticks, working, chewing on a response.

"Zepyteria will need a Matriarch in the next coming days." Father's eyes flash with crimson encircling the green of his irises. "I believe I can persuade the other royals awaiting this emergency conference we are about to engage in that you would make a most fantastic Matriarch. All I need is your cooperation. Please, help me, and I shall make you a royal."

Rhyanna skims a glance at the Knights, Mikah, and me, unsure of herself. The glamorous Fairy slips off the hand fan, slinked around her hips; twists around as she flicks it open. A flurry of daggers zips through the air, gleaming white like birds. The Knights around Mikah react too slowly; the blades plunge through the soft hollows of their throats. Mikah, however, is quicker than the eye and deflects one dagger with the sword.

Rhyanna's wings blossom out of her—inky black like a reaper crooning a death song. "Stand down, Mikah. Or I will end your life."

Mikah disregards Rhyanna's warning and ignores the fire in her eyes. Mikah advances on Rhyanna and thrusts his sword toward her abdomen. The fan-holding Fairy sidesteps the raging Fairy's near assault and glides the edges of her weapon across Mikah's midsection. Mikah drops like a stone in water, a stream of blood spilling from his stomach, his eyes losing focus.

Rhyanna, standing dangerously close to me and snaps her fan closed. "I'm sorry, Prince Nigel. One day, you will understand."

I barrel for Mikah's abandoned sword, rip it from my friend's twitching hand and go straight for Father.

Father waves his fingers at me. A wisp of green magic knocks the sword from my hand, the force powerful enough to twist my wrist. The magic works itself around me, coiling around my arms and legs. "Should you want to fight me, my son, may I suggest you drink a swig of Humans blood? It'll surely aid you on this pitiful rampage you're on. We'll put on an epic showdown before a live audience."

"You're a monster, Father," I curse as I struggle against the sorcery at work. "You slew all those innocent Fairies like the heartless beast I never imagined you to be. The Realm of Quill has fallen because of you, Father. And I shall be the Fairy to restore peace."

"How sweet of you, son, to even think such a feat is possible." My dastardly Father steps forward, his cold blue wings fluttering open. "My son, you've yet to learn all there is about what it takes to rule—what it takes to be, well, me."

"I'll never be like you. Never."

Father's wings swirl with an image of a face, warm and soft with inviting eyes and an unconditionally loving smile. Mom. "Nigel, should you want to pull the rug from my feet, I'd recommend you toss aside your inhibitions and drink. It's what Tyeese would've wanted."

I stiffen at the mention of her name. "D-did you kill Tyeese, Father?"

"Tyeese will be missed."

"Why did you do it?"

"Tyeese had eavesdropped on the conversation Matriarch Xenobia, and I were having. That alone is a crime punishable by death. But it's your fault, Nigel. You brought about this impromptu party without my knowledge. Jordana was on your side, though. She believed it'd be a great story to tell through the ages, but those pages were ripped to shreds by my brother."

Father's wings paint an image of my Mother, running, fleeing for her life. In her painted arms, she holds a baby… me.

"I was sloppy with my work," Father continues. "I would've returned to the crime scene, but time wasn't on my side." He notices my attention, following the moving art on his flapping pennons. A wicked, wicked grimace lusts upon his lips.

The murderous royal crushes his lips to my ear and sighs with immoral delight the truth of how my Mother died.

Chapter 28: Windy

I've always imagined my death would result from climbing a mound too high in the Junkyard. My foot would slip on a broken piece of scrap, and I'd come tumbling down, unable to fly because my wings are so busted up. Puff-Puff would find my body, and he'd probably take a few nibbles out of my flesh before alerting some Fairy I had perished.

I never imagined that my life would end in the water Goddess's Temple.

Abby and the Matriarch ascend the steps to the statue of Namanzi—an Ogre, not a Fairy as I had been taught. The unfortunate garlands who'd hoped to be a Prince's bride will all be sacrificed in the name of Namanzi. Madeline shouts behind the Matriarch, tugging at the determined royal's garments and pleading with her to stop. Not once has Madeline mentioned her lover should stop because innocent Fairies are about to die. Nope. All she cares about is: "Abby isn't ready."

A handful of garlands have run off, hoping to find an escape. Unfortunately, this Temple is a big loop. Another unfortunate thing: there's an enormous opening at the top of the Temple. Any Fairy wise enough would think, "I've found a way out of hell." Sadly, the twelve garlands that tried to escape were attacked by the water undulating with dead bodies in a pool at the center. The water gushed out like cephalopods limbs and plucked the Fairies from their escape and into the waiting death trap below.

I stand unmoving as the garlands shout for help and tire themselves as they run in endless circles. For a hyperactive Fairy like me, to just be still, means there's no hope. No solution. No way out. I can't read the scribbling on the walls, and I for darn sure can fly, and there isn't anything around me I can turn into a weapon.

So, I wait for death.

I hope it's quick.

"Namanzi," Matriarch Xenobia howls, her arms raised in offering as her daughter kneels in front of the Goddess, "it is time for your reign to end. No longer will you, Namanzi, hold your power over the heads of millions of Fairies. Today, Abby will draw upon your very essence and wield your might. Abby Gale Xenobia has within her veins the blood of your ancestors. It is enough that you will neither harm nor kill her, even if she is half of the very thing you hate. I call forth the powers of Namanzi in all its glory."

The statue of the water Goddess crumbles to dust. The Temple roars with energy and bursts at the seams with water like a shipwrecked vessel. Water tentacles sweep through Namanzi's home, twisting and curling, stealing away the screaming garlands and dragging them into the water. The garlands' death cries are snuffed out, replaced by gurgling sounds as they are pulled down and down and down. My feet slip in the water as I try to run, but there's nowhere to go. A water-arm loops around me, once, twice, and then uproots me like a flower.

I plummet into the sea of garlands fighting for survival and am slowly dragged to the bottom. My body bumps into other garlands who open their mouths to scream, but their songs of terror are encapsulated in a rage of bubbles.

My water-logged eyes find the sun peeking through the opening of the Temple. It watches in silence at the carnage, shining rays of gold upon us.

Something eclipses the sun. Its enormous wings block the light briefly before it swoops down. My body lets loose the breath my lungs desperately cling to, and the good night of darkness swallows me whole.

Chapter 29: Rhyanna

The story that had been written for my life by the Storytellers has become a series of blank pages. Those blank pages were once chapters that detailed the path I was to follow, guidelines that kept me loyal to a fault. My parents had completed their stories and fulfilled the contractual obligations to the royals of all the Realms. Their reward was a life of leisure, wealth, and envy. To become a Weaver, one must first be born to a family one to three degrees separated from a royal.

My lineage makes me a descendant of Crest royalty, the Realm known for its perpetual winds. The Fairies of Crest find home within the eye of storms, living in domiciles that resemble bubbles. I've traveled to my native home of Crest months before being swept away by this madness. When Matriarch Xenobia gave my parents a ring and said she was seeking garlands to accompany her to Quill, my parents informed the Matriarch they'd contemplate the offer. The "contemplating" was an unplanned journey to Crest, where my parents talked to Emerald Chandry and Topaz Lila. The Emerald and Topaz were surprised by what Prince Nigel of Quill had written for his Kingdom. They thought to interfere, to chat with King Nigel II; however, they collectively agreed that doing such wouldn't be in Crest's best interest.

Unlike Mikah and all the other Weavers who had been lied to, I had uncovered the truth long ago that my Grandmama was half Ogre. Grandmama had confessed it on her deathbed, much to the shock of all around her. From then on, I questioned everything on my unrelenting journey to know who I truly am and my purpose for being.

It drove me mad...

Now, all I want is peace.

It was an immense load to bear every waking day, prattling with friends, fellow Weavers, and all those unsuspecting of the truth: I had Ogre blood within me. Ogres were the originals of Nasturtium. That we Fairies are sealed inside of Nasturtium like ants in a jar.

Emerald Chandry and Topaz Lila give me a knowing nod from across this arena. I flash them a smile, all too aware of the story they will soon write for their Realm. Although marrying a Prince is no longer a vital part of my story, that does not mean I am to fade into the background. King Nigel's declaration that Zepyteria will need a Matriarch in a few days has me eager to pull some strings with the Emerald and Topaz.

This arena of concentric circles had been constructed by the royals of days past of stone and Human bones. At the center, King Nigel Cloud II pummels his son, Prince Nigel, with the wrath that is magic. There are cheers as the King tosses his son like a ball and laughter as the Prince fumbles to gain control of the new but temporary powers he now harbors. The Prince doesn't know what to do with it. How to control it. How to summon a deflective shield as the King's magic comes crashing down on him.

Prince Nigel appears to be distracted by all that is around him: the Human male he had to cut down like a tree to steal a drink and the words his father said to him that stirred up a rage I've never seen. In his agony and fury, Prince Nigel had agreed to have his first sip of Human blood. The Prince swore on his life to kill the King. But, given how this bloody bout is going, I doubt the Prince will be able to fulfill his patricidal desire.

A momentary pause comes to the battle, to all the commotion as wave after wave of ten-foot-tall icicles rushes into the field. Fairies all around flutter up and out of harm's way, confused by the icy spears that divide the Deep into two.

Prince Nigel bellows a haunting noise. I look down at the center to witness an exchange of power. King Nigel Cloud II has been impaled by a lone icicle, his body juddering from the unwelcome cold and the lull of death. I turn away from the fight and follow behind the procession of curious Fairies out of the mouth of the Deep. The Deep is located at the furthest reaches of Nasturtium, right on the cusp of its floral edge. There's a standstill above; every Fairy stares into the distance, baffled.

I gasp. My breath clouded with frost.

Nasturtium is an icy wonderland.

This was unscripted.

"They're escaping!" a Fairy yells. "The Humans are escaping!"

Chapter 30: Leopoldo

Windy lies snug in my arms, her brown face deprived of its earthy colors. Had I come a second late, had I not stopped whatever ceremony was transpiring, Windy would be gone. However, on my crusade to save her, I made a grave error...

That Fairy-Ogre child was in the process of making an incredible connection with a being powerful beyond explanation. I interrupted the conjuring as I went on a rampage to destroy the Ruler of Zepyteria. The child reached for her Mother—not with her hands but with a power that almost ensnared me. It was of frost and rage. Heaven and hell. The child's war song foretold my downfall by her cold, little hands.

I must dispose of that frost wielder before she finagles a way out of Nasturtium. Before an unprecedented war comes to Azolla.

My role as a savior has cost me my Dragonborn abilities. The seal on Nasturtium would not budge as I tried to bring Windy to safety. I had to call upon my brothers, Pa, and Stepmother to aid me in my desperation. They didn't believe it was worth the risk... until I offered them collateral. In retrospect, despite the cost, I think this is what they wanted all along.

Now, high in the ether of Nasturtium, the seal has been cracked. If the Fairies ever discover the fracture in their world... the Garden will be plagued by Fairies after nearly a millennium since their confinement. Pa and Stepmother have sent a band of Thaumaturgists to resolve the issue. Stepmother believes it's a waste of effort given that the newer generations of Fairies are unaware of the other Fleurs outside of their own. The Fairies seem to think their world is the only creation worthy of the Gods' time.

Windy is the first Fairy to find rest in Azolla in over a thousand years. The Fairies before her were a warmongering, bloodthirsty plague of a species.

I hear the victory chants from this high up in the Alcazar of Azolla—the skyrise home of the exalted Lucious the Cunning and Erakna the Marvelous. The skyboard, a hovering rectangle of light and sound, displays the face of the one responsible for murdering hundreds of Dragonborn: Gladius Drake. It's only fair that Gladius Drake pays for his crimes and the dissolution of a marriage.

In the years to come, I pray Windy will forgive me for the deed I've done. To us, Dragonborn, Gladius is a monster... but to Windy, she knows him as Father.

As Edward Breeze.

Acknowledgments

Wind in the Clouds was an adventure to write! Honestly, the idea is partly inspired by my 11th-grade English teacher, Mrs. Hartman, who had said something to the effect of "There aren't enough Black Fairies" for her to collect. Now, my memory is kind of fuzzy on if she had said Angels or Fairies, but nevertheless, Windy was born that day. Unbeknownst to me.

I would like to express my deepest gratitude to all who've helped make Wind in the Clouds a success in my eyes.

To my husband: I'd like to thank my husband, Corry, for listening to me ramble about the endless possibilities of where I could take this story. He is the one I go to explain my nonsensical ideas to. Even though he listens (or tries to, at least), Corry has relayed to me some epic ideas that have made their way into the Wind in the Clouds Universe.

To my Beta Readers: Linda L, Paulaesmo, and Coffeeringedits, thank you so much for the much-needed feedback that has shaped my story into something solid. Without the input of my Beta Readers, I'd have massive plot holes and static characters. I am happy to have shared this story with you all. Thank you.

To my editor: Belle Manuel, thank you for sprucing up my novel so that it can shine like a star. I appreciate you taking the time to read, reread, and edit my story until it was ready for the limelight.

To my family: I apologize for isolating myself in favor of writing. I am writing because of you all. I want to make everyone proud of everything I do and will do.

I'd like to take this final portion to thank myself. No, not in an egotistical way! But in a way that brings a smile to the face of my younger self. You are worthy, brilliant, intelligent, sassy, and funny. There were times in our life when we wanted to give up, and I am here to tell you that it does get better. As cheesy as that sounded when we were younger because we could not see the bigger picture, I am here to tell you that it does get better. Give it time.

Thank you to all who've picked up a copy of Wind in the Clouds. I hope you enjoyed the story and are prepared for more to come.

With love
-C.J. Canady

Author's Note

Wind in the Clouds came to life all on its own. The story started as mere tinkering sounds, as you've read in Windy's first chapter. I knew that the main character would be someone who loves working with their hands. The story took a considerable turn from what it would have been. Originally the story was going to be about a Fairy who goes on a wild adventure with a Prince to save the Fairy world from Ogres. In essence, the story is still the same, but with significant changes to the plot.

Many of the characters have stayed the same. But Puff-Puff was supposed to be Windy's pet—not a cursed Dragon-man named Leopoldo. That idea seemed to flow with the story beautifully. Abby was to have her own set of chapters, which I deleted after figuring out that her story didn't go well with the course of events. Abby will, however, play a huge role later in the series.

In essence, the story is about going beyond your comfort zone. A standard that I must hold myself to, as well. Windy loved to be in her Junkyard, surrounded by the familiarity of it. When she is snatched away from her safety bubble, she discovers she can exist outside her safe haven. Prince Nigel and Leopoldo are also drawn away from all the things they've come to know and love. Prince Nigel discovers that he has Ogre blood running through his veins and that Ogres—the beasts he thought them to be—are actually seeking to reclaim what was once theirs. Leopoldo went from the riches of Azolla to being cursed to roam the Fairy world in the body of a balloon Dragon.

My characters are an extension of me: living magical lives in fantastical worlds that only exist within my mind. Most of the secondary characters are loosely based on people I've met, classmates, and old friends.

By the way, Nasturtium, the collective name of the five Fairy realms, is based on the flower of the same name. But with a twist...

That will be revealed in the forthcoming book.

The cover image used for this book is not the original. Although I fell in love with the original artwork, I believe the book required an illustration that would darken the tone of what to expect from this book. The original cover, though cute, gave the book more of a kid-friendly vibe. And kid-friendly is not what I was going for.

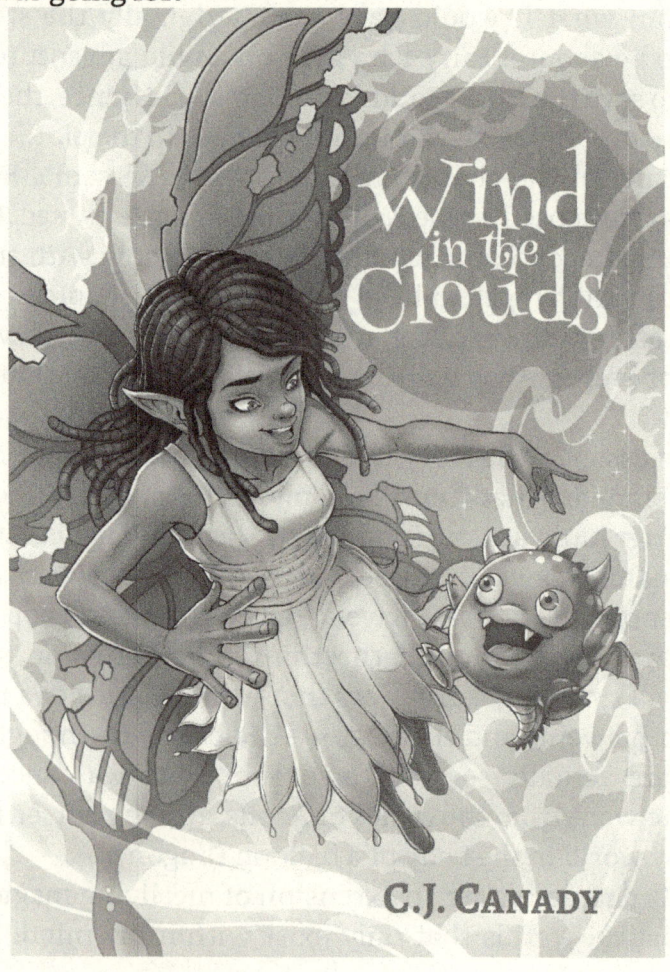

About The Author

C.J. Canady lives their everyday life in a fantasy world of endless possibilities. Dragons, Ghouls, Witches and Wizards, Space Pirates and Aliens, and cuddly sidekicks are the stars of C.J.'s novels and novellas. C.J.'s books are written in an enchanting, bewitching style that will teleport all readers to realms, dimensions, and Star Systems they'll fall desperately in love with.

C.J. hopes to one day work as a writer full-time.
You can follow them on
Instagram: Lovechrissyrobbins
Twitter: Phantasmalbook
Facebook: CJWritesBooks

Of Thorns and Hexes

A Dark Fantasy Novella by C.J. Canady

A Pricked Finger. A Drop Of Blood. A Fate Sealed.

A dark fantasy with a tragic ending and a hint of horror, "Of Thorns and Hexes" redefines gothic fantasy and offers a fresh take on the fantasy novels of old.

In the town of Yardenfeld, Elyse Allium lives a miserable life.

Living with her wicked mother, she slaves away at the local tavern in the hope that she can save enough gold to make it on her own and leave the town behind forever. However, when her mother announces that she will marry a horrible man, and is pregnant with his child, Elyse realizes she doesn't have enough time to prepare. During her last shift at the tavern, before she plans to run away, she is approached by a strange woman, a witch name Vahilda. Vahilda tells Elyse that she, too, is a witch and gives her an opportunity to leave Yardenfeld. But when Elyse declines her offer, Vahilda warns Elyse that she will die the following day.

The next morning, Elyse is preparing to run away when she is attacked by her soon-to-be stepfather. In a panic, she kills him, using powers she had never been aware of. But it's too late, and Elyse is set to be executed that night.

Before she can be killed, Elyse takes Vahilda's offer, signing a blood oath. From there, she is brought to Parnissi, where she will be trained by Vahilda for the Flower Trials. But Vahilda is not truly a friend and has an evil plan that will bring about the end of the world.

Cosmic Threads

A Dark Fantasy Novel by C.J. Canady

—Even darksome sorcery can't break a sacred bond—

Dhalia native Ashanti Orun is a Light Witch with a green thumb. One morning while tending her garden, the sky is split asunder, and a legion of winged invaders lay waste to Ashanti's village. She has the chance to save her daughter, but only by stripping young Aaliyah Orun of her vital powers. Parnissi, a subterranean world, will offer refuge to those in need, but nothing there is as it seems. A decade downstream, Aaliyah is preparing for her first day of Scavenging. The world above has fallen to ruin, aswarm with malevolent monsters. Though Aaliyah is ashamed to be magicless, she's mastered the ways of a Ghadreel Staff, hoping to use the weapon against the winged invaders. Led to her birthplace by the voice of her late mother, Aaliyah, amidst her virgin quest, unravels a network of truths that spell grave danger. Parnissi's ruler, Zeracheal Duth'Kaar, came to Earth in search of the Dragon Scale, an enchanted sword . . . but having failed to capture it, the world's last Wizard has aligned with wicked forces to achieve his ultimate sinister goal. Despite a heavy handicap, Aaliyah must embrace her fate, and help to save the Earth at last—a job that will call for faithful friends and the power of love!

C.J. Canady

Made in the USA
Las Vegas, NV
03 February 2025